Knight Squad

A novelization by David Noble

Lulu Press

Knight Squad

Copyright © 2024 Noble Park Films, LLC

Printed in the United States of America

First Edition

ISBN 979-8-9910855-4-0

Manufactured by Lulu Press, Inc.

700 Park Offices Drive Suite 250 Research Triangle, NC 27709

www.lulu.com

For information about permission to reproduce selections from this book, contact Noble Park Films at info@nobleparkfilms.com

Prologue
Korea – A Brief History

In the summer of 1950, the Korean Peninsula erupted
into conflict. North Korean forces, emboldened by the
support of the Soviet Union, surged across the 38th
parallel into South Korea. The world watched as the
Cold War turned hot on Asian soil. The United States,
still reeling from World War II, found itself drawn into
another far-flung conflict. Leading a United Nations
coalition, American troops arrived to defend South
Korea. Under the command of the ambitious General
Douglas MacArthur, UN forces executed a daring
amphibious landing at Incheon, turning the tide of the
war. As UN troops pushed northward, nearing the
Chinese border, a new player entered the fray. China,
fearing a US-aligned state on its doorstep, sent waves
of soldiers southward. These "volunteers," as China
called them, pushed the UN forces back in a series of
brutal winter battles. The war settled into a bloody
stalemate along the 38th parallel. For three more years,
the conflict raged on, neither side able to gain a decisive
advantage. Finally, in the summer of 1953, an armistice
was signed. The guns fell silent, but no peace treaty
followed. In the North, Kim Il-Sung emerged from the
war with his grip on power firmly intact. He set about
reshaping North Korean society, building a personality
cult around himself and his family. His Juche ideology
of self-reliance became the guiding principle of the
state, isolating North Korea from much of the outside
world.

The Korean War left deep scars on the peninsula and beyond. It intensified the Cold War, reshaped Asian geopolitics, and left Korea divided - a split that endures to this day. The conflict may have ended in stalemate, but its echoes continue to resound through history, a stark reminder of the human cost of ideological struggle. In the sweltering summer of 1994, North Korea stood still. The nation's ever-present loudspeakers, usually blaring propaganda, fell silent. On July 8th, the news finally broke: Kim Il-sung, the country's "Great Leader" since its founding, had died of a heart attack at the age of 82. For many North Koreans, it was as if the sun itself had been extinguished. Kim had ruled for nearly half a century, his image and words omnipresent in daily life. The country plunged into a state of collective mourning, with wailing crowds filling the streets of Pyongyang.

As the nation grieved, all eyes turned to Kim Jong-il, the deceased leader's son. For years, the younger Kim had been groomed as his father's successor, slowly accumulating power behind the scenes. Now, at 53, his moment had come. But Kim Jong-il did not immediately step into his father's role. Instead, he oversaw a three-year mourning period, solidifying his position and purging potential rivals. The country, already isolated, turned further inward. A devastating famine struck, claiming hundreds of thousands of lives, yet the regime's grip remained iron-tight. In 1997, Kim Jong-il finally assumed the title of General Secretary of the Workers' Party of Korea. The following year, he was declared "Supreme Leader." The transition was

4

complete, and a new era of dynastic rule had begun. Under Kim Jong-il, North Korea's isolationist policies intensified. He pursued a "military-first" doctrine, channeling the nation's scant resources into nuclear weapons development. International tensions rose as North Korea conducted missile tests and, in 2006, its first nuclear test.

Domestically, Kim Jong-il maintained his father's cult of personality while crafting his own. State media portrayed him as a renaissance man - a prolific writer, a musical genius, and a golf prodigy. His birthday became a national holiday, celebrated with elaborate festivals. The regime's propaganda machine worked overtime to present Kim Jong-il as the natural successor to his father's legacy. Paintings and statues of both Kims appeared side by side across the country. The message was clear: the son was the living embodiment of the father's will. As the millennium turned, North Korea under Kim Jong-il remained an enigma to the outside world. The country teetered between crisis and bellicosity, with periodic negotiations over its nuclear program interspersed with provocative actions. Kim Jong-il's rule would last until his death in 2011, marking another generational shift in North Korea's leadership. But the foundation laid during his rise to power - the seamless continuation of the Kim dynasty, the deepening of the personality cult, and the pursuit of nuclear weapons - would continue to shape North Korea's trajectory for years to come.

As winter descended upon Pyongyang in December 2011, North Korea once again found itself at a crossroads. Kim Jong-il, the "Dear Leader," had died suddenly of a heart attack. The news sent shockwaves through the country and around the world. All eyes turned to his youngest son, Kim Jong-un, a relatively unknown figure in his late twenties. Kim Jong-un's rise to power was swift and calculated. Despite his youth and inexperience, the regime's propaganda machine quickly went to work, portraying him as the spitting image of his grandfather, Kim Il-sung - the revered founder of North Korea. State media showed the young Kim inspecting troops, touring factories, and giving "on-the-spot guidance," mirroring the leadership style of his predecessors.

Within days of his father's death, Kim Jong-un was declared the "Great Successor." He assumed the titles of Supreme Commander of the Korean People's Army, First Secretary of the Workers' Party of Korea, and Chairman of the Central Military Commission. The message was clear: the Kim dynasty would continue uninterrupted. As Kim Jong-un consolidated power, he faced challenges both internal and external. Domestically, he purged potential rivals, most notably his uncle Jang Song-thaek, who was executed in 2013. Internationally, he pursued an aggressive stance, accelerating North Korea's nuclear and missile programs. Across the 38th parallel, South Korea watched these developments with a mix of concern and hope. The Republic of Korea (ROK), as it's officially known, had transformed itself from a war-torn country into an economic powerhouse and vibrant democracy.

The contrast with the Democratic People's Republic of Korea (DPRK) in the north could not have been starker.

The division of the Korean peninsula, a legacy of the 1950s war, remained as entrenched as ever. The Demilitarized Zone (DMZ), a misnomer for one of the most heavily fortified borders in the world, continued to separate the two Koreas. Families torn apart by the war remained divided, with only rare, emotional reunions organized by the two governments. Under Kim Jong-un, North Korea's approach to South Korea and the wider world oscillated between provocation and dialogue.

In 2018, in a surprising turn of events, Kim Jong-un met with South Korean President Moon Jae-in at the DMZ, stepping across the border in a symbolic gesture. This was followed by unprecedented summits with U.S. President Donald Trump. Yet, despite these diplomatic overtures, fundamental differences remained. North Korea clung to its nuclear program, viewing it as essential for regime survival. South Korea, backed by the United States, insisted on denuclearization as a precondition for any substantial change in relations.

As of 2024, the Korean peninsula remains divided. In the North, Kim Jong-un continues to rule with an iron fist, maintaining his family's cult of personality while pursuing economic reforms and nuclear deterrence. In the South, democracy continues to flourish, with the country playing an increasingly prominent role on the world stage. The stark contrast between the two Koreas serves as a living testament to the long shadow cast by the Cold War. Two nations, one people, separated by history and ideology, continue to eye each other across a fortified border. The dream of reunification, once fervently held by many on both sides, seems more distant than ever. Yet history has shown that change can come swiftly and unexpectedly on the Korean peninsula. As a new generation comes of age with no personal memory of a unified Korea, the future of this divided land remains uncertain, a geopolitical puzzle that continues to challenge the world's diplomats and policymakers.

Chapter 1
Prison Break

The warehouse loomed in the darkness, its vast interior barely illuminated by the faint glow of external lights filtering through grimy windows. Suddenly, a long rope snaked down from the ceiling, its end hitting the concrete floor with a soft thud. Preybird, a lithe figure clad in black, rappelled down the rope with practiced ease. Her boots touched the ground silently as she landed in a crouch, her keen eyes scanning the shadowy expanse around her. Every muscle in her body was taut, ready for action. Without wasting a moment, she moved swiftly through the warehouse, her steps light and purposeful. As she approached a corner, the sound of voices made her freeze. Preybird pressed herself against the wall, holding her breath as two Korean military guards passed by, their laughter echoing in the empty space.

"이 야간 근무는 정말 지루해," one guard said in Hangeul, complaining about the boring night shift.

"그래도 월급은 좋잖아," the other replied with a chuckle, reminding his companion about their good pay.

As soon as they were out of sight, Preybird darted down the adjacent corridor, her heart racing. She knew her window of opportunity was narrow. Reaching a secure area, she pulled out a crumpled piece of paper from a hidden pocket and quickly punched a code into the control panel. The door unlocked with a soft click, swinging open. Preybird reached into her gear, extracting a black hood. Taking a deep breath, she stepped through the doorway. Moments later, she emerged, but she wasn't alone. A hooded figure stumbled beside her, clearly disoriented and possibly drugged. Time was running out. Preybird gripped the arm of her companion, pulling them along as she retraced her steps. But as they rounded the corner, her blood ran cold. There, blocking their path, stood the two military guards she had evaded earlier.

For a heartbeat, time seemed to stand still. Preybird's mind raced, calculating her options as the guards' expressions shifted from surprise to alarm. She knew that in the next instant, all hell would break loose. The guards' eyes widened in shock, their hands fumbling for their weapons. But Preybird was already in motion. With lightning speed, she shoved the hooded man aside, her body coiling like a spring. In a blur of calculated violence, Preybird struck. Her fist connected with the first guard's solar plexus, driving the air from his lungs. As he doubled over, she pivoted, her elbow smashing into the temple of the second guard. Both men crumpled to the floor, unconscious before they hit the ground.

Preybird stood over their fallen forms, her chest heaving slightly. She allowed herself only a moment to survey the damage, her mind already racing ahead to the next phase of her mission. Grabbing the arm of the hooded man, who had slumped against the wall, she continued down the corridor at a brisk pace. The pair rounded another corner, approaching a heavy metal door. Preybird's boot connected with it, the sound of impact echoing through the hallway as the door flew open. She dragged her disoriented companion through the threshold, her senses on high alert. Suddenly, a piercing wail cut through the air. Sirens blared from all directions, bathing the facility in pulsing red light. Preybird's head snapped up, her eyes narrowing as she scanned their surroundings. The sound of multiple footsteps and shouted orders in Korean reached her ears.

"에어리어 봉쇄! 침입자를 찾아라!" The command to lock down the area and find the intruders rang out.

Preybird's mind raced. Their escape route was rapidly closing. She could hear the heavy boots of security guards converging on their location from multiple directions. The hooded man beside her swayed unsteadily, a liability in the chaos that was about to unfold. With grim determination, Preybird tightened her grip on her companion. She had come too far to fail now. As the sounds of pursuit grew louder, she made a split-second decision, veering off towards a narrow side passage. It was time to improvise.

The next few moments would determine whether her daring rescue would end in triumph or disaster. Preybird's muscles tensed, ready for the fight of her life. The narrow passage opened into a wider area, and Preybird's heart sank. Multiple doors burst open simultaneously, and heavily armed ROK military guards poured in from every direction. Within seconds, she and the hooded man were surrounded, the barrels of numerous weapons trained on them. Preybird's mind raced, assessing the situation. The odds were overwhelming. In a swift motion, she released her grip on the hooded man, who collapsed to the ground with a dull thud. She took a deliberate step away from him, her body language shifting subtly. A man with more elaborate insignia on his uniform stepped forward, clearly the leader of the security detail. His eyes raked over Preybird's form, a mixture of surprise and condescension in his gaze.

"무기를 내려놓아라. 그냥 여자애일 뿐이다. 우리가 한 여자애 정도는 감당할 수 있어!" he barked in Hangeul, his voice dripping with misplaced confidence.

Preybird, understanding Korean, felt a surge of grim amusement at his words: "Drop your weapons. It is just a girl. We can handle one girl!"

To her surprise, the security leader's order was followed. One by one, the guards lowered their weapons to the ground, their eyes never leaving her. The tension in the room shifted palpably. Beneath her mask, Preybird's lips curled into a smile. These men had just made a catastrophic error in judgment, one she was about to exploit ruthlessly. In that moment of false security, Preybird's body coiled like a spring. Her mind cleared, time seeming to slow as she plotted out her next moves. The guards had underestimated her, seeing only a woman where they should have recognized a deadly operative. Their mistake would be her opportunity. Preybird knew she had mere seconds to turn this seemingly hopeless situation to her advantage. Her eyes darted around, marking each guard's position, noting potential weapons and escape routes.

The security leader barely opened his mouth to speak again when Preybird immediately launched into action. The next few seconds would be a whirlwind of violence, a deadly dance that would determine not only her fate but that of the mysterious hooded man at her feet. In a blur of motion, Preybird exploded into action.

13

The security guards, caught off-guard by her sudden movement, scrambled to react. But Preybird was already among them, a whirlwind of deadly precision. She ducked under the first guard's wild swing, using his momentum to throw him into two of his comrades. As they tumbled to the ground, Preybird was already moving, her elbow connecting with another guard's solar plexus, doubling him over.

The fight became a chaotic dance, with Preybird at its center. She leapt, spun, and twisted, always one step ahead of her opponents. When three guards rushed her simultaneously, she dropped low, sweeping the legs out from under one while using another as a human shield against the third's attack. Preybird's acrobatic skills came into play as she vaulted over a guard, landing behind him to deliver a knockout blow. She used the environment to her advantage, bouncing off walls and using fallen guards as impromptu weapons. The number of conscious opponents dwindled. The security leader realized the grave error in his judgment. With desperation in his eyes, he lunged for his discarded weapon. Time seemed to slow as he raised the gun, aiming at Preybird.

The crack of gunfire echoed through the room. But Preybird was ready. In a move that seemed to defy physics, she snatched a fallen metal plate from the ground, using it as a makeshift shield. Bullets ricocheted off the plate with metallic pings. In one fluid motion, Preybird produced a knife from a hidden sheath. The blade glinted in the harsh light as it spun

14

through the air. The security leader's eyes widened in shock, a look frozen on his face as the knife found its mark with deadly accuracy. Silence fell over the room. Preybird stood among the fallen guards, her chest heaving slightly from exertion. She surveyed the scene, confirming that none of her opponents would rise again.

Her attention turned to the hooded man, still lying where she had left him. Muffled whimpers emanated from beneath the hood, a reminder of her mission's purpose. Preybird approached the man cautiously, her mind already racing ahead to their escape. The alarms still blared in the distance, a warning that their window of opportunity was rapidly closing. She reached down towards the hooded figure, knowing that the most dangerous part of her mission was still to come. The fight might be over, but the real challenge of escaping this facility with her vulnerable charge was just beginning. Preybird moved swiftly, her every motion efficient and purposeful. She hauled the hooded man to his feet, supporting his weight as he swayed unsteadily. The sound of screeching tires cut through the air, and Preybird's head snapped towards the noise.

A nondescript van came barreling around the corner, its engine roaring as it bore down on their position. In one smooth motion, Preybird yanked open the van's side door and unceremoniously shoved the hooded man inside. He tumbled onto the floor of the vehicle with a muffled grunt. Without hesitation, Preybird leapt in after him, pulling the door shut behind her. "Go!" she barked at the unseen driver. The van's tires squealed as it peeled away from the scene, leaving behind the chaos of the warehouse. The van sped through the night. Preybird allowed herself a moment to catch her breath. The hooded man lay still on the floor, his chest rising and falling rapidly. Their escape had been narrow, but they weren't in the clear yet.

Unknown to Preybird and her team, they had an observer. High above the warehouse floor, behind a reflective window pane, a shadowy figure had witnessed the entire event. Sharp eyes had taken in every detail of the fight, the rescue, and the escape. As the van disappeared into the night, the figure stepped back from the window, melting into the darkness of the room. The observer's mind was already racing, analyzing the implications of what they had just seen.

This mysterious watcher, known only as Sasha, realized that the night's events were merely the opening move in a much larger game. As Sasha retreated from the window, plans were already forming, strategies being calculated. The escape of Preybird and her hooded charge might have seemed like a success, but it had set in motion a chain of events that would have far-reaching consequences. As dawn broke over the city, the true complexity of the situation was only beginning to unfold.

Chapter 2
Street Fight

The driverless subway car hummed as it sped through the dimly lit tunnel, its rhythmic motion a stark contrast to the stillness of its lone passenger. Daniel sat slumped next to the window, his forehead resting against the cool glass. His eyes were fixed downward, unseeing, lost in thought. A battered satchel lay at his feet, its worn leather a testament to years of use. Daniel's disheveled appearance spoke volumes - his wrinkled shirt and loosened tie painting a picture of a man going through the motions, his spirit dampened by the weight of routine.

The artificial voice of the subway's announcement system crackled to life, jarring Daniel from his reverie. "다음 역은 중앙역입니다. 내리실 문은 오른쪽입니다," it declared, its cheery tone at odds with Daniel's mood.

The Korean announcement, translating to "The next station is ChongAng Station. The doors will open on the right," echoed through the car.

With a deep sigh, Daniel lifted his head. His tired eyes flicked to the digital screen displaying the upcoming stops. Recognition dawned on his face - this was his cue. Mustering what little energy he had, Daniel pushed himself to his feet. He swayed slightly as the subway car decelerated, one hand reaching out to steady himself against a nearby pole. As the doors slid open with a soft hiss, he bent down to retrieve his satchel, slinging it over his shoulder with practiced ease. Daniel shuffled out of the car, his feet dragging slightly as he joined the small crowd making their way towards the exit. The fluorescent lights of the station cast harsh shadows across his face, accentuating the dark circles under his eyes. He approached the staircase leading to the street level, each step feeling heavier than the last. As he climbed, the sounds of the city above grew louder - car horns, snippets of conversation, the general bustle of urban life.

Finally, Daniel emerged from the subway exit, squinting as the bright daylight assaulted his eyes. He paused for a moment, taking in the familiar sights and sounds of the city street. With a resigned set to his shoulders, he merged into the flow of pedestrians, another face in the crowd heading to another day at work. As Daniel trudged up the subway exit stairs, his mind was already at his desk, dreading another day of monotonous work. The city sounds grew louder with each step, but something unusual cut through the typical urban cacophony. Thwacks, grunts, and muffled shouts reached his ears. Daniel paused, his brow furrowing. These weren't the normal sounds of the bustling city street. His grip tightened instinctively on his satchel as he cocked his head, trying to pinpoint the source of the disturbance.

Curiosity overcame his usual apathy. Daniel quickened his pace, taking the remaining steps two at a time. As he neared the top of the staircase, the noises intensified. He could now make out the unmistakable sounds of a violent struggle. Daniel reached the edge of the staircase and froze, his eyes widening in shock at the scene before him.

The usually busy sidewalk had transformed into a battleground. Two distinct groups of men were locked in a fierce brawl, their actions a blur of savage intensity. On one side were men in street clothes, their accents and occasional shouts marking them as Russian. Opposing them were men in slacks, ties, and jackets – now disheveled from the fight – who Daniel recognized as Korean from their features and bursts of angry Hangeul. The air was filled with the dull thuds of fists meeting flesh and the sharp clangs of improvised weapons. A Russian wielded a broken bottle, its jagged edges glinting in the morning sun. A Korean man parried with a briefcase, using it as both shield and bludgeon.

Blood spattered the concrete as a knife found its mark. Someone screamed in pain. The violence was raw, desperate, and utterly out of place in the morning rush hour. Daniel stood transfixed, his mouth agape. This was no simple street brawl – the coordinated movements and ferocity of both sides spoke of something more organized, more dangerous. He was witnessing a clash between the Russian and Korean mobs, their hidden underworld suddenly and violently spilling onto the streets. As the reality of the situation sank in, Daniel's instincts screamed at him to flee. But his feet seemed rooted to the spot, his eyes unable to tear away from the brutal spectacle unfolding before him. In that moment of paralysis, Daniel didn't realize that his presence hadn't gone unnoticed. Amidst the chaos, a pair of cold eyes had locked onto him, marking him as a witness to something he was never meant to see.

Daniel's heart raced as he pressed himself against the cold metal of the light pole, trying to make himself as small as possible. The sounds of the brawl filled his ears - the meaty thwacks of fists connecting, the sharp cries of pain, the angry shouts in Russian and Korean. From his vantage point, Daniel scanned the chaotic scene. His eyes darted from one violent exchange to another, his mind struggling to process the brutality unfolding before him. Then, amidst the mayhem, he spotted something that made his blood run cold. On the far side of the street stood a young girl, no more than ten years old. She was frozen in place, her small hands clutching a backpack to her chest. The child's eyes were wide with terror, fixed on the violence that raged between her and safety. Daniel's breath caught in his throat. The fighting was spreading, moving dangerously close to where the girl stood. In moments, she could be caught in the crossfire.

Without conscious thought, Daniel's body sprang into action. Self-preservation gave way to a surge of protective instinct. He darted out from behind the light pole, his feet pounding against the pavement as he raced towards the child. "Hey!" he shouted, trying to catch the girl's attention over the din of the fight. "Get down!" The young girl, SuJin, stared in silence.

As he ran, Daniel's mind raced through possible escape routes. The subway entrance was blocked by the brawl. The sidewalk to his left was a gauntlet of flying fists and flashing blades. Their only hope was to reach the alley he'd spotted just beyond where the girl stood. Daniel's lungs burned as he pushed himself harder, acutely aware of every second ticking by. He could see the girl more clearly now - her school uniform, her pigtails, the tears streaming down her face. She hadn't moved an inch, paralyzed by fear. Daniel's head snapped towards the sound, spotting a frantic mother on the other side of the fight, reaching out helplessly towards her daughter.

With a final burst of speed, Daniel closed the distance to SuJin. He scooped her up in his arms, feeling her small body trembling against his chest. "I've got you," he panted. "Hold on tight!"

Cradling SuJin protectively, Daniel spun on his heel, ready to make a dash for the alley. But as he turned, he found himself face to face with one of the mob enforcers, the man's cold eyes locking onto him with deadly intent. Daniel's mind raced. He had saved the girl from immediate danger, but now they were both trapped in the middle of a war zone. As Daniel turned to flee with SuJin, a hulking figure broke away from the main brawl. Boris, a brute of a man with a shaved head and a face marred by old scars, had spotted Daniel's dash across the battlefield. With a predator's focus, he abandoned his current opponent and charged towards Daniel and the girl.

"Hey!" Boris bellowed, his thick Russian accent cutting through the chaos. "Where you think you're going?"

Daniel's eyes widened as he saw the mountain of muscle barreling towards them. There was no time for hesitation. In one fluid motion, he grabbed SuJin's small hand, his fingers wrapping protectively around hers.

"Run!" Daniel shouted, tugging the girl alongside him as he sprinted towards the narrow alley he had spotted earlier. SuJin stumbled at first, her short legs struggling to keep up with Daniel's desperate pace.

Boris roared in frustration, shoving aside both friend and foe as he pursued his new targets. His heavy footfalls echoed off the buildings, growing louder with each passing second. Daniel's lungs burned as he pushed himself to run faster. He could feel SuJin's hand trembling in his grasp, hear her panicked breathing.

The alley entrance loomed ahead, a dark mouth promising either sanctuary or a dead end.

"Almost there," Daniel gasped, more to himself than to SuJin. He risked a glance over his shoulder and immediately wished he hadn't. Boris was closing the gap, his face contorted with rage.

With a final burst of speed, Daniel and SuJin plunged into the alley. The sounds of the street fight became muffled, replaced by the echoes of their footsteps and ragged breathing bouncing off the close walls. The alley was a maze of shadows, littered with obstacles - discarded boxes, overflowing dumpsters, forgotten debris. Daniel navigated them as best he could, pulling SuJin along, praying he wasn't leading them into a trap.

Behind them, Boris crashed into the alley entrance, his bulk barely fitting through the narrow passage. "You can't hide!" he bellowed, his voice reverberating off the walls.

Daniel's mind raced. They couldn't outrun the man forever. He needed a plan, a way to lose their pursuer in this urban labyrinth. As they rounded a corner, Daniel spotted a half-open door leading into one of the buildings. Without breaking stride, he made a split-second decision. It was a risk, but it was their only chance.

"This way," he whispered to SuJin, guiding her towards the door. "Quick and quiet."

As they slipped through the doorway into the unknown interior of the building, Daniel could only hope he had made the right choice. The sounds of Boris's pursuit grew closer, and Daniel knew that their impromptu escape was far from over. Daniel and SuJin burst into the alley, their rapid footsteps echoing off the narrow walls. The passage was a stark contrast to the bustling street they'd left behind - dingy and claustrophobic, lined with overflowing trash crates and illuminated by the eerie glow of flickering neon signs. As soon as they were a few yards in, Daniel dropped to one knee in front of SuJin, his hands gently grasping her shoulders.

Daniel's eyes scanned her quickly for any signs of injury, his breath coming in ragged gasps. "Are you okay?" he asked instinctively, concern etched across his face.

SuJin stared back at him, her eyes wide with fear and confusion. She shook her head slightly, not understanding his words. Daniel mentally kicked himself, realizing his mistake in the heat of the moment. He paused, racking his brain for the correct Korean phrase. It had been years since his language classes, but he knew he had to try. SuJin's safety depended on clear communication.

Taking a deep breath, Daniel spoke again, this time in halting Korean. "괜찮아요?" he asked, hoping his pronunciation was close enough to be understood.

Relief washed over him as SuJin's expression changed. She nodded slowly, comprehending his question. Though she affirmed she was physically unharmed, the fear in her eyes told Daniel she was far from okay.

"It's alright," Daniel said softly in English, before catching himself and switching back to his limited Korean. "괜찮아요," he repeated, trying to infuse the words with as much reassurance as he could.

SuJin's small frame trembled slightly, her hands clutching the straps of her backpack like a lifeline. The sounds of the fight they'd escaped were muffled now, but still audible - a reminder that danger wasn't far behind. Daniel's mind raced. They couldn't stay here long. Boris would be searching for them, and this alley, while providing temporary shelter, was ultimately a dead end. They needed a plan, fast.

As he opened his mouth to speak again, a crash echoed from the entrance of the alley. Daniel's head snapped towards the sound, his body tensing. Had Boris found them already?

In that moment, Daniel knew their brief respite was over. Whatever came next, he had to protect this scared little girl who had been thrust into his care by circumstance. With determination setting his jaw, he turned back to SuJin, ready to guide her through the next phase of their escape. Daniel reached into his pocket, his fingers closing around a familiar piece of cloth. He pulled out a handkerchief adorned with colorful, cartoonish animals - a memento from a happier time he kept as a good luck charm.

Offering it to SuJin with a gentle smile, Daniel spoke softly, "Here. Take this. Just think about the happy animals and everything will be alright."

Though she couldn't understand his words, SuJin seemed to grasp his intent. She took the cloth, her small fingers tracing the playful designs. For a brief moment, a smile flickered across her face, a ray of sunshine breaking through storm clouds. But the respite was short-lived. SuJin's eyes suddenly widened in terror, fixed on something behind Daniel. The smile vanished from her face as quickly as it had appeared. Daniel felt his stomach drop as a massive shadow fell over them. He turned slowly, already knowing what he would see. Boris loomed at the entrance of the alley, his hulking frame blocking out the light, a malevolent grin spreading across his scarred face. Time seemed to slow as Boris charged. Daniel had just enough time to push SuJin behind a stack of crates before the Russian's meaty fist connected with his jaw. The force of the blow sent Daniel sprawling, his vision exploding with stars. He scrambled to his feet, tasting blood in his mouth. Boris was already on him again, a flurry of punches raining down. Daniel managed to block some, his office worker's physique no match for the mobster's brute strength. He fought desperately, not for victory, but for survival - for SuJin's safety.

Just as Daniel's strength began to fail, a blur of motion caught his eye. A new figure had entered the fray, launching himself at Boris with precision and power. The newcomer, a man Daniel would later know as Robert, moved with the fluid grace of a trained fighter. Robert's fist connected with Boris' temple, staggering the big Russian. A swift kick to the knee brought Boris down, and a final, decisive blow left him sprawled on the alley floor. Boris, dazed and outmatched, scrambled to his feet. With a last hateful glare at Daniel and Robert, he turned tail and ran, disappearing into the maze of city streets. Daniel sagged against the alley wall, his breath coming in ragged gasps. He looked at Robert with a mixture of gratitude and wariness. Who was this man? And how had he known to intervene?

Robert knelt down to SuJin's level, his face etched with concern. The tenderness in his expression contrasted sharply with the efficient violence he had just displayed. "I told you not to be out here alone. You know it's not safe," carried a mix of relief and gentle admonishment.

SuJin's lower lip trembled as she nodded in agreement. The fear in her eyes was replaced by a look of contrition, and she lowered her gaze, clutching Daniel's cartoon handkerchief tighter. Robert pulled SuJin into a protective embrace, his strong arms enveloping her small frame. She buried her face in his shoulder, her body relaxing slightly in the safety of his presence.

After a moment, Robert turned to face Daniel, his arms still around SuJin. His eyes, sharp and assessing, softened with gratitude. "Thank you for protecting my sister," he said in English, his accent barely noticeable.

Chapter 3
A Brother's Protection

Daniel, still slumped against the alley wall, could only manage a weak nod in response. The adrenaline that had fueled his desperate flight was fading fast, leaving him acutely aware of the pain pulsing through his body. His jaw throbbed where Boris had landed his first punch, and he could feel the sting of various cuts and bruises forming. He tried to push himself up, but a sharp pain in his ribs caused him to gasp and slide back down. The world swam before his eyes, and he blinked hard, trying to focus.

"Your sister?" Daniel finally managed to croak out, his voice rough. "I... I'm glad I could help. Is she okay?"

Robert nodded, giving SuJin one last squeeze before standing up. His brow furrowed as he took in Daniel's condition. "She will be, thanks to you."

As if to emphasize his point, a distant shout echoed down the alley, followed by the sound of running feet. The mob fight was spreading, searching for new battlegrounds.

Robert's posture tensed, his eyes scanning the alley exits. "Will you be okay?" he asked.

Daniel gritted his teeth and attempted to stand once more. Pain lanced through his side, and he slumped back, breathing heavily. "I... I don't think so," he admitted, frustration and fear mixing in his voice.

Daniel sat on the grimy alley ground, his body a canvas of fresh bruises and aches. He looked up at Robert, his vision still slightly blurred from the fight. Despite the pain, a wry smile tugged at the corner of his mouth. "Thank you again."

"Su---sure. No problem," Daniel managed to stutter out, his voice raspy. He gave a small shrug, wincing as the movement sent a twinge through his battered ribs.

Robert nodded, his expression a mix of gratitude and urgency. He reached down and took SuJin's small hand in his own. The little girl clutched Daniel's cartoon handkerchief in her other hand, her eyes darting between her brother and the man who had tried to save her. As Robert turned to leave, guiding SuJin away from the scene of violence, he paused. Looking back over his shoulder, his eyes met Daniel's with a grim intensity.

"You should leave the area," Robert warned, his voice low and serious. "The Russians will be coming back for you."

The weight of Robert's words hung in the air, cutting through the fog of pain clouding Daniel's mind. The reality of his situation came crashing down - he was now a marked man in a world he barely understood. Adrenaline surged through Daniel's system once more. Gritting his teeth against the pain, he pushed himself to his feet. His legs wobbled unsteadily for a moment, but determination kept him upright. Daniel nodded in agreement, his eyes scanning the alley for the quickest escape route. Without another word, he turned and began to run, each step sending jolts of pain through his battered body. But fear and survival instinct propelled him forward, away from the danger that lurked behind.

As he fled, Daniel's mind raced. Where could he go? His apartment? Work? Both seemed woefully inadequate sanctuaries against the forces now pursuing him. The city he thought he knew had transformed into a labyrinth of potential threats. Daniel rounded a corner, leaving the alley and Robert and SuJin behind. He plunged into the bustling streets, just another face in the crowd, but carrying with him the knowledge that his world had irrevocably changed.

The ordinary day he had anticipated when he woke up that morning had vanished, replaced by a reality where every shadow could hide an enemy, and safety was now a luxury he could no longer afford.

The serene landscape of rolling mountains stretched out before Robert, a stark contrast to the chaos that had engulfed him just hours ago. He sat cross-legged on a simple bamboo mat, his eyes closed, attempting to find the inner peace that had always eluded him. The mountain air was crisp and clean, carrying the scent of pine and wild herbs. It should have been calming, grounding. Instead, Robert's mind was a tempest of fragmented memories and swirling emotions.

He tried to focus on his breathing, to clear his thoughts, but the images came unbidden:

> The clash of metal on metal as the Russian and Korean mobs collided in the street...

> SuJin's terrified face as she stood frozen, caught in the crossfire of a war she didn't understand...

> The stranger - Daniel - racing across the battlefield to sweep SuJin to safety...

Robert's eyes snapped open, his breath coming in ragged gasps. The serenity of the mountain vista seemed to mock his inner turmoil. He clenched his fists, feeling the familiar tension coiling in his muscles, ready for a fight that wasn't there.

"Dammit," he muttered under his breath, rising to his feet in one fluid motion. The bamboo mat curled at the edges as he stepped off it, no longer weighed down by his presence.

Robert began to pace, his steps sure and silent even on the uneven mountain terrain. His mind raced, replaying the events of the morning over and over. He had trained for years to protect his family, to navigate the dangerous waters of Seoul's underworld. And yet, when it mattered most, it was a stranger who had saved SuJin. The realization stung, a blow to his pride and a stark reminder of his limitations. He couldn't be everywhere at once, couldn't anticipate every threat. The thought of how close he had come to losing SuJin made his blood run cold.

And then there was Daniel. An ordinary man thrust into extraordinary circumstances. Robert had left him behind in that alley, bruised and disoriented. Had he made the right choice? Or had he simply traded one innocent life for another? Robert stopped at the edge of a small cliff, looking out over the vast expanse of mountains. The world below seemed so small, so insignificant from up here. But he knew better. Down there, in the twisted streets and shadowy alleys, a war was brewing. And he was caught in the middle of it, with too much to lose and too few allies to trust. He took a deep breath, letting the mountain air fill his lungs. The meditation might have failed, but standing here, feeling the solid earth beneath his feet and the endless sky above, Robert found a moment of clarity.

He couldn't change the past, couldn't undo the events that had led him to this point. But he could shape what came next. He had decisions to make, alliances to forge or break, and a family to protect at all costs. With renewed determination, Robert turned back towards the path that would lead him down the mountain and back into the fray. The peace he sought might be elusive, but his purpose was clear. Whatever came next, he would face it head-on. As he began his descent, a nagging thought tugged at the back of his mind. Daniel, the unexpected hero of the morning's chaos. Robert couldn't shake the feeling that their paths would cross again. For better or worse, the ordinary office worker had been drawn into a world he couldn't possibly understand. And in that world, Robert knew, there were no innocent bystanders - only survivors and victims.

The ancient pagoda stood as a silent sentinel on the mountainside, its weathered wood and faded paint telling stories of centuries past. Within its protective embrace, SuJin sat cross-legged, a colorful Korean children's book spread open on her lap. A small array of snacks lay scattered around her, a picnic of normalcy in a world that had turned upside down. SuJin's eyes danced across the pages, her lips moving silently as she

34

read. Every so often, she would reach out to grab a rice cracker or a slice of fruit, the simple act of snacking a comfort in itself. For a moment, she could pretend that this was just another day, that the terrors of the morning were nothing more than a bad dream. The sound of approaching footsteps made her look up. Robert, known to her as Jun Ho, was walking towards the pagoda, his face softening as he saw her. The tension in his shoulders seemed to ease, if only slightly, at the sight of his sister safe and engrossed in her book.

As he reached SuJin, Robert's hand darted out, quick as a snake, snatching a rice cracker from her collection. A mischievous glint appeared in his eyes, a rare break from the serious demeanor he usually wore. SuJin's face scrunched up in mock outrage. "Hey! That's mine, Jun Ho!" echoed in the quiet mountain air.

Robert's lips curled into a smile, a genuine expression that reached his eyes. It was a glimpse of the playful older brother that existed beneath the hardened exterior of a man caught between worlds.

Robert retorted in Korean, his voice tinged with challenge and affection. "What are you going to do about it?" As he spoke, he deliberately raised the stolen snack to his mouth, taking an exaggerated bite while maintaining eye contact with SuJin.

For a moment, the weight of their circumstances lifted. They were just a brother and sister, engaged in the timeless dance of sibling teasing. The pagoda, the mountain, the distant threats – all faded into the background. SuJin's eyes narrowed playfully, accepting the challenge. She lunged forward, trying to reclaim her snack, but Robert deftly moved it out of her reach. Their laughter, bright and unburdened, filled the air. As they play-fought over the stolen morsel, Robert felt a pang in his chest. These moments of normalcy were becoming increasingly rare. He wanted to freeze this instant, to protect SuJin's laughter and innocence from the harsh realities that lurked beyond their mountain refuge.

But even as he reveled in the joy of their interaction, a part of Robert remained vigilant. His eyes scanned the surrounding area, his ears attuned to any sound out of place. The world they inhabited didn't allow for complete relaxation, not even in moments like these. As their laughter subsided, Robert ruffled SuJin's hair affectionately. "What book are you reading?"

SuJin's face lit up, eager to share her current adventure in literature. As she launched into an animated description of the story, Robert settled beside her, allowing himself to be drawn into her world of imagination and wonder. For now, at least, they could pretend that this peaceful moment would last forever. But deep down, Robert knew that soon, too soon, he would have to face the challenges that awaited them in the world below. The stolen cracker, the shared laughter, the simple joy of a story – these were the moments he would hold onto, the reasons he would continue to fight. SuJin's response to Robert's teasing was swift and unexpected. With a mischievous glint in her eye, she snatched up a nearby napkin and tossed it directly at her brother's face. The paper sailed through the air, landing squarely on Robert's nose.

For a moment, Robert's eyes widened in surprise. Then, with exaggerated drama, he contorted his face into an expression of mock hurt. His lower lip jutted out in an overblown pout, his eyebrows knitting together in feigned distress. The sight was too much for SuJin. She burst into peals of laughter, the sound bright and infectious. Her small body shook with mirth, eyes crinkling at the corners as she reveled in her successful counterattack. Robert's facade cracked, a genuine smile breaking through as he watched his sister's joy. These moments of pure, unbridled happiness were all too rare, and he cherished each one.

Still chuckling, Robert settled himself next to SuJin in the pagoda. As he sat, however, his expression sobered slightly. The weight of their reality began to reassert itself. "Finish up what you're doing. We have to leave."

SuJin's laughter faded, replaced by a look of confusion and disappointment. "So early? But you just started your training," carried a note of concern.

Robert sighed, running a hand through his hair. "I know SuJin, but I can't concentrate."

The playful atmosphere from moments ago had evaporated, replaced by a tension that even SuJin, young as she was, could sense. She looked at her brother, really looked at him, noticing the tightness around his eyes, the set of his jaw. Robert forced a smile, reaching out to ruffle SuJin's hair affectionately. "Don't worry."

But even as he spoke the words, he knew they rang hollow. As SuJin began to pack up her books and remaining snacks, Robert's mind raced. The inability to find peace, even here in this secluded spot, was telling. The events of the morning – the fight, the danger SuJin had been in, the mysterious Daniel – all of it swirled in his thoughts, demanding action.

He knew they couldn't stay hidden away forever. Sooner or later, the world below would come calling, and when it did, he needed to be ready. For SuJin's sake, and for his own. Rising to his feet, Robert offered a hand to help SuJin up. As she took it, he made a silent promise to himself and to her. Whatever came next, he would face it head-on. The tranquility of the mountain had eluded him, but perhaps he would find the clarity he sought in action. "Let's go."

Together, they stepped out of the pagoda, leaving behind the brief moment of normalcy. The path ahead was uncertain, but Robert was determined to forge it, one step at a time.

As they prepared to leave, SuJin suddenly reached into her pocket, pulling out a small piece of cloth. It was the handkerchief Daniel had given her during the chaos of the previous day, its cartoonish animal designs a stark contrast to the gravity of their situation. "Maybe this will help," SuJin said softly in Korean, her voice hopeful.

Robert took the cloth from SuJin, his brow furrowing as he examined it. The soft material felt out of place in his calloused hands, a fragment of innocence in a world that had long since stripped him of his own. "Where did you get this?"

SuJin's face brightened at the memory. "From that nice man who helped me yesterday."

Robert's eyes narrowed slightly as he stared at the cloth, Daniel's face flashing in his mind. The ordinary office worker who had risked everything to save SuJin, a stranger who had shown more courage in those few moments than many hardened men Robert had known. "Nice man, huh."

SuJin, sensing her brother's conflicted emotions, tugged gently at his sleeve. "Jun Ho, you should be his friend."

Robert couldn't help but smile at SuJin's simple, heartfelt suggestion. If only the world were that easy, where alliances could be formed and trust given based on a single act of kindness. But even as he entertained the thought, he knew the reality was far more complicated. His gaze drifted to the distant horizon, his mind racing with the implications of what had transpired. Daniel was now irrevocably entangled in their dangerous world, whether he realized it or not. The Russians would be looking for him, seeing him as a loose end to be tied up. And Robert... Robert wasn't sure where Daniel fit into the complex web of loyalties and enemies he navigated daily.

The cloth in his hand seemed to carry the weight of a decision yet to be made. Could Daniel be trusted? Could he be an ally in the battles to come? Or was he simply another variable, unpredictable and potentially dangerous? Robert's fingers closed around the handkerchief, feeling its soft texture. For a moment, he allowed himself to see it through SuJin's eyes - not as a reminder of danger, but as a token of kindness, a small beacon of hope in their turbulent world.

"우리 가자," Robert finally said, carefully folding the cloth and tucking it into his pocket. "Let's go."

As they began their descent from the mountain, Robert's mind was made up. He would find Daniel again. Whether as a friend or a potential threat, he needed to understand the man who had so unexpectedly become a part of their story. The path ahead was uncertain, but Robert was determined to face it head-on, with SuJin's safety as his guiding star and the memory of an unexpected act of bravery as a compass.

Chapter 4
A Chance Meeting

The driverless subway car hummed through the darkened tunnel, its rhythmic motion a stark contrast to the turmoil in Daniel's mind. He sat slumped against the window, his reflection a testament to the ordeal he had endured. Bruises painted his face in mottled shades of purple and yellow, a painful reminder of his encounter with Boris. Daniel's battered satchel lay at his feet, a surviving relic from his old life - a life that now seemed impossibly distant. His eyes were fixed downward, unseeing, lost in the replay of yesterday's events. The memory of SuJin's terrified face, the brutal fight, and Robert's warning echoed in his mind. The car was nearly empty, the few other passengers giving Daniel a wide berth. Whether it was his disheveled appearance or the aura of barely contained anxiety he exuded, no one seemed eager to get close.

"다음 역은 중앙역입니다. 내리실 문은 오른쪽입니다," the artificial voice of the subway system announced, its cheery tone at odds with Daniel's mood. The Korean words, "The next station is ChongAng Station. The doors will open on the right," cut through his reverie.

Daniel's head jerked up, his eyes focusing on the digital display. Recognition dawned on his face, tinged with a hint of fear. This was his stop - the same station where yesterday's chaos had erupted. For a moment, he considered staying on the train, riding it to the end of the line and beyond, escaping the city and the danger it now held. But some combination of habit and resignation propelled him to his feet. He swayed slightly as the car decelerated, one hand reaching out to steady himself against a nearby pole. The motion sent a jolt of pain through his ribs, a sharp reminder of his vulnerability. The platform beyond seemed eerily normal, commuters rushing about their day as if yesterday's violence had never happened. He took a deep breath, wincing at the pain in his side, and stepped out of the car.

Daniel's feet felt leaden as he approached the staircase leading to the street level. Each step was an effort, both physically and mentally. He was acutely aware of his surroundings, his eyes darting from face to face, searching for any sign of the Russian mobsters who might be hunting him. The bright daylight assaulted Daniel's eyes. Daniel squinted, raising a hand to shield his face. The bustling street before him was a scene of ordinary urban life, but to Daniel, it now felt like a battlefield. Every passing car could be harboring enemies, every alley a potential ambush point. He stood there for a moment, paralyzed by indecision. Should he go to work, pretend that nothing had happened? Or should he run, leave everything behind and try to disappear? The weight of yesterday's choices pressed down on him, the consequences of his moment of heroism now fully apparent.

With a mix of fear and determination, Daniel merged into the flow of pedestrians. He was heading to work, but his mind was elsewhere, strategizing, planning, wondering when and where the next threat would emerge. The day ahead loomed like an uncertain battlefield, and Daniel, the reluctant warrior, was walking straight into it. Daniel emerged from the subway exit, his body tense and his senses on high alert. The memories of yesterday's violence were etched into every bruise on his body, turning the once-familiar street into a landscape of potential threats. His eyes darted from side to side, scanning the bustling sidewalk and the flow of traffic beyond. His grip on his satchel tightened unconsciously, knuckles whitening as if the worn leather could offer some protection against unseen dangers.

For a moment, he stood frozen, a statue of uncertainty amidst the river of commuters. Then, slowly, he allowed himself to breathe. The street was normal - no sign of menacing Russians or Korean gangsters, just the usual morning crowd hurrying to their destinations. Daniel took a tentative step forward, then another. Each movement was measured, deliberate. He made his way to the corner, his head constantly swiveling, checking and re-checking his surroundings. The weight of unseen eyes seemed to press down on him, though the passersby paid him no mind. At the intersection, Daniel hesitated again. The path to his office stretched out before him, a route he had walked countless times without a second thought. But today, it felt exposed, dangerous. His gaze fell on a local bar just down the street - a dingy establishment that had never before looked so inviting.

With his decision made, Daniel altered his course. The bar offered anonymity, a place to gather his thoughts and perhaps fortify himself with some liquid courage before facing the day ahead. He moved towards it with purpose, unaware that his every step was being watched. High above the street, a figure stood motionless in the shadows of a rooftop. Sharp eyes tracked Daniel's progress, noting the office worker's nervous demeanor and unexpected detour. The game of cat and mouse had begun, though Daniel remained oblivious to his role as the mouse. The watcher on the roof was merely one piece on a much larger board, where Daniel had unwittingly become a central figure. The mysterious figure melted back into the shadows of the rooftop. The next moves in this dangerous game were about to be played, and unseen forces were positioning themselves for what was to come.

Inside the bar, unaware of the eyes that had tracked his every move, Daniel was still trying to make sense of a world that had spiraled so quickly out of control.

The bar door creaked open, admitting Daniel into a world of shadows and smoke. The stark contrast between the bright morning outside and the dim interior momentarily disoriented him. As his eyes adjusted, he took in the scene - a study in faded glory and lingering despair. The air was thick with the acrid scent of stale cigarettes and spilled beer. A few patrons hunched over their drinks, each lost in their own private miseries. The soft clink of glasses and the low murmur of hushed conversations provided a somber soundtrack to the morning's desperation. Daniel made his way to the far end of the counter, his footsteps muffled by the worn carpet. He eased himself onto a bar stool, wincing slightly as his bruised body protested the movement. His satchel found its place beside him, a faithful companion in his descent into this den of early-morning escape.

With a subtle gesture, Daniel caught the bartender's attention. "Draft beer," he muttered, his voice rough from disuse. The bartender, a man whose lined face suggested he'd seen it all, gave a noncommittal grunt and moved to fulfill the order.

Daniel swiveled on his stool, his eyes sweeping the bar. It was a habit born of his newfound paranoia, a constant need to assess his surroundings for potential threats. But instead of danger, his gaze landed on something unexpected. At the other end of the counter sat a woman. Even in the dim light, Daniel could see she was striking - and jarringly out of place in this gloomy establishment. Her presence was like a splash of color in a grayscale world. Daniel found himself looking again, this time with more curiosity. There was something about her that didn't quite fit - a youthfulness that seemed at odds with her world-weary posture. He wondered about her age, about what series of events could have led someone like her to be drowning her sorrows at this hour.

Sensing his scrutiny, the woman - Jessica - glanced in his direction. It was a fleeting look, barely more than a flicker of her eyes, but it was enough to send a jolt through Daniel. In that brief moment of eye contact, he saw a reflection of his own turmoil, a kindred spirit in the chaos that had become his life. Jessica's gaze returned to her drinks - three empty shot glasses stood as silent testimony to her own battles. Her fingers toyed with the rim of a fourth, still full, as if debating whether to continue her descent or claw her way back to sobriety.

Daniel's beer arrived with a dull thud on the counter. He wrapped his hand around the cool glass, grateful for something tangible to hold onto. Daniel's eyes drifted back to Jessica. In the space between them, heavy with unspoken stories and shared desperation, Daniel felt a strange connection forming. Two strangers, each bearing their own invisible wounds, finding a moment of silent understanding in the most unlikely of places. Daniel couldn't shake the feeling that this chance encounter was somehow significant. In a world that had suddenly become unpredictable and dangerous, even the smallest connection felt like a lifeline.

Daniel's heart sank as he watched Jessica's face contort with disgust. He turned away, unable to bear the sight of her rejection. The worn wooden counter of the bar beckoned, promising solace in the form of his half-empty beer bottle. A weary sigh escaped his lips as he gripped the cool glass. The amber liquid inside sloshed gently, a stark contrast to the turmoil in his mind. Suddenly, unbidden memories flooded his consciousness.

> The alley. The smell of rotting garbage. Boris's leering face, illuminated by the harsh glow of a lone streetlight. The glint of a knife. The sickening crunch of knuckles meeting flesh.

Daniel's fingers tightened around the bottle. With a sharp movement, he slammed it down onto the counter. The hollow thud echoed through the dim bar, loud enough to turn heads but not quite forceful enough to shatter the thick glass. Jessica whirled around at the sound, her eyes wide with a mixture of surprise and concern. She opened her mouth to speak, but the words died on her lips as she took in Daniel's rigid posture and clenched jaw.

Lost in his own dark thoughts, Daniel barely registered Jessica's reaction. His mind raced, replaying the attack over and over. He was so engrossed in his memories that he nearly jumped out of his skin when a hand clamped down on his shoulder. "You shouldn't be so jumpy," a familiar voice chuckled from behind him.

Daniel spun around, his heart pounding, to find Robert grinning at him. The older man's weathered face was creased with amusement, but there was a glimmer of worry in his eyes. "Christ, Robert," Daniel muttered, willing his racing pulse to slow. "Give a guy some warning next time."

Daniel spun around, his eyes widening with a mixture of surprise and excitement. The adrenaline from his earlier fright morphed into a strange, buzzing energy. "What is it with you?" he blurted out, a hint of a grin tugging at the corner of his mouth. "You some sort of sadomasochist junky?"

Robert's weathered face crinkled with amusement, his eyes twinkling mischievously. "I don't know what that is," he chuckled, "but if it makes you feel better at night, then yes!" He paused, his expression shifting to something more cryptic. "My name is Jun Ho."

Daniel blinked, his brow furrowing in confusion. The playful atmosphere evaporated, replaced by bewilderment. "What?" he asked, his voice tinged with disbelief.

Robert — or Jun Ho — seemed to realize his mistake. He waved a hand dismissively, as if trying to erase his previous statement from the air. "Jun Ho... never mind," he said quickly. "Just call me Robert."

The bizarreness of the exchange left Daniel momentarily speechless. He turned back to the bar, lifting his beer bottle to his lips. The cool liquid offered a welcome distraction from the odd turn in conversation. After taking a long swig, he set the bottle down and faced Robert again.

"So," Daniel began, deciding to ignore the strange name revelation for now, "how is your little friend?"

Robert's face softened, a hint of gratitude creeping into his voice. "You mean my sister SuJin? She's fine. I wanted to thank you for trying to save her the other day."

Daniel's eyebrows shot up, indignation flaring in his chest. "What do you mean 'try'?" he retorted, his voice rising slightly. "I rescued that girl!"

Robert held up his hands in a placating gesture, a smirk playing at the corners of his mouth. "Okay, if you say so," he conceded, though his tone suggested he wasn't entirely convinced.

Daniel opened his mouth to argue further but found his attention drawn elsewhere. His gaze drifted across the bar to Jessica, who seemed determined to ignore their conversation. She sat rigidly on her stool, her back to them, nursing a drink of her own.

Robert followed Daniel's line of sight, his smirk deepening as he noticed the younger man's distraction. "You should avoid that one," he advised, his voice low and knowing.

Daniel leaned in closer, his words barely above a whisper. "I think she's too young to be in here."

Robert snorted, amusement dancing in his eyes. "What are you, her father?"

The jab hit home. Daniel felt his face flush with embarrassment, and he sank a little lower in his chair. He took another swig of his beer, using the bottle to hide his reddening cheeks.

Daniel couldn't help but notice the subtle shift in Robert's demeanor. The older man's eyes darted around the room, as if checking for eavesdroppers. The air between them seemed to thicken with unspoken tension.

Daniel leaned in slightly, lowering his voice. "Everything okay? You seem... different tonight."

Robert's gaze locked onto Daniel's, a mixture of wariness and determination in his eyes. "It's complicated," he murmured. "But that's actually why I'm here. I need your help with something..."

A flicker of movement caught Robert's attention. His eyes darted up to a television monitor mounted above the bar. The sound was muted, but the grim-faced newscaster's lips moved rapidly, accompanying images of crime scenes and flashing police lights.

Robert's expression darkened as he watched the report. "Looks like things are getting worse out there," he muttered, more to himself than to Daniel.

Daniel followed Robert's gaze, his own face growing serious as he took in the images on the screen. "Yeah," he agreed quietly. "It's like the whole city's going to hell."

Robert tore his eyes away from the TV, fixing Daniel with an intense stare. "That's actually why I wanted to talk to you," he said, his voice low and urgent. "Things are worse than they seem, and I think you might be the only one who can help."

Daniel straightened in his chair, intrigued despite his better judgment. "What are you talking about, Robert?"

Without waiting for a response, Robert stood and made his way to the exit, leaving Daniel to stare after him in confused anticipation. Daniel found himself torn between curiosity and caution. Whatever Robert wanted to show him, he had a feeling it would change everything. The television above the bar suddenly caught Daniel's full attention. The muted screen flickered with violent images: shadowy figures exchanging gunfire in narrow alleys, police cordoning off blood-spattered sidewalks, and grim-faced detectives examining chalk outlines. A banner at the bottom of the screen proclaimed in bold letters: "Mob violence intensifies in Seoul".

The bartender, noticing Daniel's interest, reached for the remote and unmuted the TV. The newscaster's voice, tinged with barely concealed alarm, filled the now-quiet bar:

"There has been a steep rise in violence in the Seoul metropolitan area. Many officials speculate that the increase has been contributed by the growing mafia presence. One insider source has gone so far as to say that the internal turmoil may be too much for the authorities to handle."

A chill ran down Daniel's spine as he processed the information. The city he'd come to know and love was descending into chaos, and he felt powerless to stop it.

Robert's gravelly voice cut through Daniel's thoughts. "All I care about is protecting my sister."

Daniel turned to respond, but Robert was already moving, his broad shoulders tense as he strode purposefully towards the exit.

"Yeah, you're welcome!!!" Daniel called after him, his voice a mixture of frustration and sarcasm. The words echoed in the bar, drawing curious glances from the other patrons.

Daniel was left with a nagging sense of unfinished business. The gratitude Robert had expressed earlier now felt hollow in light of his abrupt departure. Daniel turned back to his beer, his mind racing. The news report, Robert's cryptic behavior, the mysterious sister – it all swirled together in a confusing mix. He couldn't shake the feeling that he was on the edge of something much bigger and far more dangerous than he'd realized. He glanced over at Jessica, wondering if she'd overheard any of his conversation with Robert. She remained stubbornly focused on her drink, but Daniel noticed a slight tension in her shoulders that hadn't been there before.

Daniel couldn't help but feel that his next decision would be crucial. The violence in Seoul was escalating, and somehow, he seemed to be caught in the middle of it all. With a deep breath, Daniel made up his mind. He drained the last of his beer, slammed the bottle on the counter with perhaps more force than necessary, and stood up. Whatever Robert was involved in, whatever was happening in this city, Daniel was determined to find out. And maybe, just maybe, he could do something to help. Daniel cast one last glance at the TV. The images of violence had been replaced by a weather forecast, but the newscaster's words still rang in his ears. The streets of Seoul were no longer safe, and

Daniel was about to step right into the heart of the storm.

Chapter 5
Sasha's Tale

The mid-afternoon sun cast long shadows across the bustling streets of Seoul. Among the modern high-rises and neon signs, one building stood out - a gaudy, brightly lit establishment with Cyrillic lettering proclaiming its name. The Russian club was a jarring reminder of the city's increasingly diverse and sometimes dangerous underbelly. Boris, a hulking figure in a tailored suit that did little to hide his muscular frame, strode purposefully down the sidewalk. His cold eyes scanned the area, a habit born from years of watching his back. Satisfied that he wasn't being followed, he approached the club's entrance. The bouncers, mountain-like men themselves, straightened imperceptibly as Boris neared. With a curt nod, he pushed past them and disappeared into the pulsing darkness beyond the door.

Just as the door swung shut behind Boris, a petite figure rounded the corner. SuJin, her school uniform crisp despite the long day, clutched the straps of her backpack tightly. Her eyes, wide with a mixture of fear and determination, darted around the street before settling on the Russian club's garish facade.

She froze mid-step, her breath catching in her throat as she recognized Boris's retreating form. Time seemed to stand still as she watched him enter the club, her mind racing with the implications of his presence. For a moment, SuJin stood rooted to the spot, indecision written across her young face. Then, as if a spell had been broken, she spun on her heel. Her backpack bounced wildly as she broke into a run, her footsteps echoing off the buildings as she fled the scene. The street, momentarily disrupted by this small drama, quickly returned to its usual rhythm. Pedestrians continued their journeys, oblivious to the undercurrents of danger and intrigue that had just played out before them. But for SuJin, running as fast as her legs could carry her, the world had shifted. She knew something now - something important, something dangerous - and she had to tell someone before it was too late.

As she ran, dodging surprised pedestrians and ignoring their irritated calls, SuJin's mind was focused on one thing: finding her brother. Robert needed to know what she had seen. And maybe, just maybe, they could figure out a way to stop whatever was coming before it tore their world apart. The Russian club receded into the distance behind her, its gaudy lights a beacon of the growing darkness in Seoul. But SuJin didn't look back. She couldn't afford to. Not when time was running out, and the stakes were higher than ever.

Inside the Russian club, the atmosphere was thick with tension and cigarette smoke. The dim lighting cast long shadows across the faces of the gathered men, their features hardened by years of violence and suspicion. The air hummed with low murmurs and the occasional clink of ice in glasses filled with amber liquid.

At the center of it all stood Nicholi Volkov, his imposing figure elevated above the rest on a small platform. His piercing gaze swept across the room, commanding attention without uttering a word. The assembled men, an assortment of muscle-bound enforcers and sharp-eyed strategists, all bore the unmistakable look of the Russian mafia. Boris shouldered his way through the crowd, ignoring the grumbles and dirty looks shot his way. He took his place near the back, his eyes narrowing as he tried to gauge the mood of the room.

Nicholi's voice, deep and gravelly, cut through the murmurs like a knife. "So what we have been hearing for some time is in fact true," he declared, his words hanging heavy in the air. "Our comrade Sasha here witnessed the entire thing." He gestured to a nervous-looking man standing nearby. "Sasha, come here and tell everyone."

As Sasha hesitantly made his way to the front, Boris leaned towards the thug next to him. "What is Nicholi talking about?" he whispered, his curiosity getting the better of his usual stoic demeanor.

The man beside him remained silent, his eyes fixed on Nicholi. Boris felt a flicker of annoyance, but he knew better than to push further. In this room, asking the wrong questions could be deadly. Sasha reached Nicholi's side, his face pale in the dim light. He cleared his throat, his eyes darting nervously around the room before settling somewhere over the heads of the assembled men.

"I... I saw them," Sasha began, his voice trembling slightly. "The Jopok. They're mobilizing. Gathering weapons, recruiting new blood. They're preparing for war."

A low murmur rippled through the crowd. Boris felt his muscles tense, his hand instinctively moving towards the concealed weapon at his side. The Jopok - the Korean mafia - had long been a thorn in their side, but open warfare? This was unprecedented.

Nicholi raised a hand, silencing the whispers. His face was a mask of cold fury. "We've ruled this city for years," he growled. "We will not be pushed out by these upstarts. It's time we remind them who truly owns these streets."

As Nicholi continued to outline their retaliation plans, Boris's mind raced. The violence that had been simmering beneath the surface of Seoul was about to boil over. And he was caught right in the middle of it. How much danger were they in? Boris listened intently, committing every detail to memory. But a part of him couldn't shake the feeling that this conflict was bigger than any of them realized. The Russian club, once a symbol of their power and influence, now felt like a war room. And as Boris looked around at the hardened faces of his comrades, he knew that the streets of Seoul were about to become a battlefield. Sasha stepped forward, his shoulders hunched as if trying to make himself smaller under the weight of Nicholi's gaze. The room fell into an expectant hush, the air heavy with anticipation. Nicholi gave a curt nod, granting Sasha permission to speak. The smaller man took a deep breath, his eyes darting nervously around the room before he began his tale.

"Teell them the other part," Nicholi ordered.

"I was at my post, trying to get information on the Korean military as ordered," Sasha started, his voice gaining strength as he spoke. "It was quiet as usual, until..." He paused, swallowing hard. "Until a woman broke in and attacked the entire compound."

A ripple of disbelief ran through the crowd. Boris leaned forward, his brow furrowed in confusion. Sasha continued, his words tumbling out faster now. "She took out the entire unit! And then I saw him..." His voice dropped to a near whisper, forcing everyone to strain to hear. "He is still alive. With my own eyes I saw him, I know it was him. He still lives!"

For a moment, the room was eerily silent as the implications of Sasha's words sank in. Then, like a dam bursting, chaos erupted. The far end of the room exploded into a cacophony of shouts and curses. Men leapt to their feet, faces contorted with rage and disbelief. Glasses shattered as they were hurled against walls. The air became thick with cigarette smoke and the acrid scent of spilled vodka.

"Impossible!"

"He's lying!"

"We killed him ourselves!"

The roar of voices grew louder, drowning out individual words into a sea of fury and fear. Boris stood silent amidst the storm, his mind racing. Who was this mysterious "he" that had survived? And who was the woman capable of taking down an entire unit? Through the haze of smoke and shouting, Boris caught sight of Nicholi. The leader stood motionless on his platform, his face an impassive mask. But in his eyes, Boris saw something he'd never seen before: a flicker of genuine fear.

As the uproar continued, Boris felt a chill run down his spine. Whatever -- or whoever -- Sasha had seen, it was clear that the game had changed. The carefully maintained balance of power in Seoul was about to be shattered, and the resulting chaos would engulf them all.In that moment, as the angry shouts of his comrades faded into a dull roar in his ears, Boris made a decision. He needed to find out more. About this mysterious survivor, about the woman who had single-handedly taken down a military compound, about the true extent of the threat they were facing. As the meeting devolved into heated arguments and frantic planning, Boris slipped away unnoticed. The streets of Seoul awaited, and with them, the answers he sought. The city was a powder keg, and the fuse had just been lit. Night had fallen over Seoul, casting long shadows across the narrow alleyways that wound between the traditional Korean homes. The modern city seemed a world away in this quiet neighborhood, where tiled roofs and wooden doors spoke of an older, more peaceful time.

The stillness of the evening was suddenly broken by the sound of rapid footsteps. SuJin burst into the alley, her school uniform disheveled and her breath coming in short, sharp gasps. Her backpack bounced wildly against her back as she ran, her eyes wide with urgency. She darted between the closely packed houses, her feet sure on the familiar path despite the dim lighting. The warm glow of paper lanterns hanging from eaves cast fleeting shadows across her face as she passed, highlighting the mixture of fear and determination in her expression. Finally, SuJin skidded to a stop in front of one particular home. It was indistinguishable from its neighbors to the casual observer, but to SuJin, it was a beacon of safety in a world that had suddenly become much more dangerous.

She paused for a moment, bent over with her hands on her knees, trying to catch her breath. The weight of what she had witnessed outside the Russian club pressed heavily on her young shoulders. She knew she had to tell her brother, had to warn him about Boris and whatever nefarious plans the Russian mafia was hatching. With one final deep breath, SuJin straightened up and approached the door. Her hand trembled slightly as she reached out to knock, the enormity of the situation finally catching up with her now that she had stopped running. As her knuckles met the worn wood of the door, SuJin couldn't shake the feeling that everything was about to change. The quiet alley, the traditional home, the normal life she had known - it all felt suddenly fragile, like a soap bubble on the verge of bursting.

She knocked again, more urgently this time. "Oppa!" she called out, using the respectful term for her older brother. "Robert! Please, open up! It's important!"

The seconds stretched into an eternity as SuJin waited, shifting nervously from foot to foot. The information she carried felt like a physical weight, a ticking time bomb that needed to be defused. Finally, she heard movement from inside the house. As the sound of approaching footsteps reached her ears, SuJin steeled herself. Whatever happened next, whatever dangers lay ahead, she knew that this moment - this breathless, adrenaline-fueled dash through the streets of Seoul - was the point of no return.

SuJin remembered the key. above the door frame. Looking around to make sure no one was around, she slyly reached up and found the key, pulling it down and unlocking the door. The door began to open, and SuJin prepared herself to unleash the torrent of information she had been holding back. The peaceful alley held its breath, unaware that it was about to become the stage for revelations that would send shockwaves through the underworld of Seoul. The interior of the Korean home was a haven of calm, suffused with the warm glow of traditional paper lamps. The air was rich with the aroma of homemade soup, a comforting scent that seemed at odds with the tension about to enter.

Robert, known to most as Jun Ho, sat cross-legged on a cushion at a low table. He lifted a spoon of steaming soup to his lips, savoring the familiar flavors that reminded him of simpler times. For a moment, the weight of his double life - Robert to some, Jun Ho to others - seemed to lift from his shoulders. The peaceful scene shattered as the door burst open. SuJin flew into the room like a whirlwind, her school uniform askew and her face flushed from running. Her eyes, wide with a mixture of fear and excitement, locked onto her brother.

SuJin exclaimed in rapid-fire Korean, her words tumbling out in a breathless rush. "I saw them! Jun Ho, I saw them!"

Robert's instincts kicked in immediately. He set down his soup bowl with deliberate calm, his eyes never leaving his sister's face. Years of training allowed him to maintain an outward appearance of tranquility, even as his mind raced through possible scenarios.

Robert rose smoothly, crossing the room in a few quick strides to reach SuJin. Gently, he placed his hands on her shoulders, his touch meant to both comfort and steady her. "Who did you see?"

SuJin took a deep breath, trying to calm herself under her brother's steadying gaze. The contrast between them was stark - SuJin, all nervous energy and urgency, and Robert, a picture of careful control. SuJin continued in Korean, her voice dropping to a whisper as if afraid the very walls might be listening. "The Russians. I saw them going into the club. Something big is happening, brother."

Robert's expression remained neutral, but a muscle twitched in his jaw. He guided SuJin to the table, gesturing for her to sit. "Slow down, sister. Tell me everything, from the beginning."

SuJin's chest heaved as she struggled to regain her composure. Her eyes, wide with residual fear, locked onto her brother's face. She took a deep breath, steadying herself before speaking again. "Those foreigners that attacked me last week. They were near my school."

The words hung in the air, heavy with implication. Robert's body visibly tensed, his casual demeanor evaporating in an instant. He stood abruptly, turning away from SuJin as if to hide the storm of emotions crossing his face. For a moment, the only sound in the room was the soft ticking of a clock and SuJin's gradually steadying breaths. Robert's mind raced, connecting dots and foreseeing consequences with the speed and precision of a chess grandmaster.

When he turned back to face SuJin, his expression was a mask of determination. His eyes, usually warm and comforting, now held a steely glint that SuJin had rarely seen. Robert kept his voice low and intense. "SuJin, show me."

SuJin blinked, momentarily taken aback by the shift in her brother's demeanor. This wasn't the easygoing Robert she was used to seeing around the house. This was Jun Ho - the man she glimpsed only in fragments, the one who moved in shadows and spoke in whispers. SuJin stammered, glancing nervously at the darkened windows. "R-right now?"

Robert nodded curtly. "Now is best. Before it's too late."

He moved with purpose, retrieving a jacket from a nearby hook and shrugging it on. As he did, SuJin caught a glimpse of something metallic at his waist - a sight that sent a shiver down her spine. SuJin scrambled to her feet, her exhaustion forgotten in the face of this new urgency. As she followed her brother out into the night, she couldn't shake the feeling that she had set something enormous in motion - something that might be beyond even her brother's control. The quiet street seemed different now, charged with potential danger. Robert moved with a predator's grace, his eyes constantly scanning their surroundings. SuJin struggled to keep up, both physically and mentally, as they retraced her earlier path.

As they walked, Robert spoke quietly, his words meant for SuJin's ears alone. "SuJin, you were very brave. But from now on, you need to be more careful. What we're dealing with isn't just simple criminals."

The Russian club loomed ahead, its gaudy lights a beacon in the night. Robert's hand moved instinctively to his side, and SuJin's fears were confirmed - her brother was armed "I'll go alone from here," Robert said softly. "You go back home. Lock the doors and don't let anyone in."

As SuJin opened her mouth to protest, Robert silenced her with a look. In that moment, she saw not just her older brother, but a man standing on the precipice of a dangerous world - a world he had clearly been part of for longer than she had realized. "Be careful, brother."

Chapter 6
A Squad is Formed

The night air was thick with tension as the neon lights of the Russian club cut through the darkness. The establishment stood out like a sore thumb in the Seoul streetscape, a beacon of foreign influence and underworld activity. Huddled against the wall near the club's entrance was a figure that seemed to melt into the grime of the city. Han, dressed in tattered layers that spoke of a life lived on the streets, sat motionless, his eyes hidden beneath a grimy cap. To the casual observer, he was just another unfortunate soul, invisible in the bustle of city life. The club's door swung open, spilling out a mix of pulsing music and raucous laughter. Boris and Sasha emerged, their expensive suits a stark contrast to the figure huddled nearby.

Their eyes, sharp and calculating, immediately zeroed in on Han.

Boris approached with purposeful strides, his face twisting into a sneer of disgust. Without hesitation, he swung his foot, connecting with Han's shabby shoes. "Hey, bum," Boris growled, his accent thick with contempt. "Get moving... you don't belong here."

Han stirred, his movements slow and deliberate as he raised his head to meet Boris's gaze. For a brief moment, something flickered in Han's eyes - a spark of intelligence, of purpose - but it was gone so quickly one might have imagined it.

Rising to his feet with exaggerated difficulty, Han shuffled backwards, hands raised in a placating gesture. He mumbled in Korean, his voice rough and slurred. "Sorry, I meant no trouble."

Boris and Sasha watched with narrowed eyes as Han stumbled away, their postures relaxing only slightly as the perceived threat retreated. They exchanged a meaningful glance, unspoken communication passing between them. As if on cue, the club's door burst open again. This time, a stream of men poured out, all bearing the unmistakable look of the Russian mafia. They moved with urgent purpose, splitting off in different directions as soon as they hit the street. From his peripheral vision, Han observed this exodus. His stumbling gait slowed almost imperceptibly, his head tilting just enough to track the movements of the departing Russians. To anyone watching, it would have appeared as nothing more than a drunk's unsteady progress.

But Han was far from drunk. Behind the facade of a homeless vagrant, his mind was racing. The sudden departure of so many high-ranking members, the tension evident in their hurried movements - something big was happening, and Han knew he needed to report it. As he shuffled further away from the club, Han allowed himself a small, grim smile. His disguise had worked perfectly, allowing him to gather crucial intelligence right under the noses of some of Seoul's most dangerous men.

Now, as he meandered through the darkened streets, Han's thoughts turned to his next move. The information he'd gathered needed to be passed on quickly. The balance of power in Seoul's underworld was shifting, and Han knew that every second counted. With one last glance over his shoulder to ensure he wasn't being followed, Han ducked into a narrow alley. In the shadows, his posture straightened, his movements becoming swift and sure. The transformation was startling - where moments ago there had been a stumbling drunk, now stood a man of purpose and skill. Han reached for a concealed phone, his fingers flying over the keypad as he composed a coded message. As he hit send, he knew that wheels were being set in motion - wheels that would soon bring the various factions of Seoul's criminal underworld into a collision course. With his mission accomplished, Han melted deeper into the maze of

Seoul's back streets. The night was still young, and there was much more work to be done.

The bar was a study in shadows and secrets. Smoke hung in the air like a shroud, twisting lazily in the dim light. The clink of glasses and the low murmur of conversation provided a constant backdrop, punctuated occasionally by the harsh bark of laughter or the scrape of a chair. Daniel hunched over the bar, his fingers wrapped around a sweating bottle of beer. His eyes, slightly unfocused from the alcohol, scanned the room for what felt like the hundredth time. He was searching for a familiar face, but the sea of strangers remained unbroken.

As he turned back to his drink, a sudden weight crashed down on his shoulder. Daniel's body tensed, adrenaline surging through his system as he whirled around, nearly toppling off his barstool.

Robert stood behind him, a mischievous grin playing at the corners of his mouth. "A bit jumpy, are we?"

Daniel's heart hammered in his chest as he tried to regain his composure. "Seriously!" he exclaimed, his voice a mix of exasperation and relief. "Do you really enjoy freaking me out, Robert?"

Robert's grin widened as he slid onto the stool next to Daniel. He signaled the bartender for a drink before turning back to his flustered companion. "Maybe you should really sit at a booth," he suggested, his tone lighthearted but with an undercurrent of seriousness. "No one can sneak up on you with your back to the wall."

Daniel snorted, taking a long pull from his beer. "What, are you my personal safety instructor now?"

Robert's expression sobered slightly. He leaned in closer, his voice dropping to a near-whisper. "In this city, you need to be careful. Eyes are everywhere."

The sudden shift in Robert's demeanor sent a chill down Daniel's spine. He studied his companion's face, noting the tension around his eyes, the slight furrow of his brow. "Robert," he began hesitantly, "what's going on? You seem... different tonight."

Robert's gaze swept the bar, taking in every patron, every darkened corner. When he turned back to Daniel, his eyes were hard, all traces of earlier amusement gone. "Things are changing, Daniel," he said, his voice low and urgent. "The balance is shifting, and I'm not sure anyone is ready for what's coming."

Daniel felt a knot forming in his stomach. The cryptic warning, combined with Robert's uncharacteristic intensity, painted a picture he wasn't sure he wanted to see. "What are you talking about? What balance?"

Robert glanced around once more before leaning in even closer. "Listen carefully," he whispered. "There are forces at work in this city that you can't even imagine. The Russians, the Jopok... they're all making moves.

And caught in the middle of it all are people like you and me."

Daniel's mind reeled. "Me? What do I have to do with any of this?"

Robert's hand tightened on Daniel's shoulder. "More than you know," he said grimly. "That girl you rescued... my sister... you've become a part of this whether you wanted to or not."

A chill ran down Daniel's spine as the implications of Robert's words sank in. The bar suddenly felt too small, too exposed. "What do we do?" he asked, his voice barely audible over the ambient noise of the bar.

Robert stood, his eyes constantly scanning their surroundings. "For now, you stay alert. Trust no one. And Daniel..." he paused, waiting until he had Daniel's full attention. "Be ready. When the time comes, I may need your help." Daniel couldn't shake the feeling that he was standing on the edge of something vast and dangerous - a world hidden just beneath the surface of the Seoul he thought he knew.

Robert's expression shifted, a smirk playing at the corners of his mouth. His eyes gleamed with a mix of amusement and something darker, more urgent. He leaned in, his voice dropping to a conspiratorial whisper. "Daniel, it's getting *really* crazy outside, and we should *really* be doing something about it."

The repetition of 'really' hung in the air between them, charged with unspoken meaning. Daniel felt a flicker of irritation, tinged with defensiveness. "I already did," he retorted, his voice tight. "I called the police on those thugs."

Robert's eyebrows rose, a challenge in his gaze. "And what came of that?"

The question hit Daniel like a punch to the gut. He lowered his head, unable to meet Robert's eyes. "Nothing," he muttered, the word tasting bitter on his tongue.

"Exactly," Robert said, his voice hard. "Nothing happened. And I for one am sick of it!"

In one fluid motion, Robert stood, his hand closing around Daniel's arm. Before Daniel could protest, he found himself being steered towards a booth in the corner of the bar. The vinyl seat creaked as they slid in, the high backs of the booth providing a cocoon of relative privacy.

Robert leaned across the table, his eyes intense. "Look, Daniel," he began, his voice low and urgent. "The system is broken. The cops, the courts - they're all either too scared or too corrupt to do anything about what's really going on in this city."

Daniel felt a chill run down his spine. He'd suspected as much, but hearing it stated so bluntly was jarring.

"So what are you suggesting?" he asked, a note of trepidation in his voice.

Robert's lips curved into a grim smile. "I'm suggesting we take matters into our own hands. No more sitting on the sidelines, no more hoping someone else will fix things. It's time we did something."

The weight of Robert's words hung heavy in the air between them. Daniel's mind raced, a mix of fear and excitement coursing through him. Part of him wanted to dismiss Robert's words as the ramblings of a man who'd had too much to drink. But another part - a part that had been growing steadily since his encounter with the Russian thugs - resonated with the call to action.

"What exactly did you have in mind?" Daniel asked, surprised by the steadiness in his own voice.

Robert's eyes gleamed with approval. He leaned in even closer, his voice dropping to barely above a whisper. "First, we gather information. We need to know who the major players are, what they're planning. Then, we start disrupting their operations. Small stuff at first, but enough to let them know they're not untouchable."

As Robert laid out his plan, Daniel felt a shift within himself. The Seoul he thought he knew was falling away, revealing a darker, more dangerous city beneath.

And yet, instead of fear, he felt a growing sense of purpose.

"I'm in," Daniel said, the words leaving his mouth before he'd fully processed them. "Whatever it takes, I'm in."

Robert nodded, a look of grim satisfaction on his face. "Good," he said. "Because once we start down this path, there's no turning back. Are you sure you're ready for that?"

Daniel met Robert's gaze, his jaw set with determination. "I'm sure," he said. "It's time someone did something. Might as well be us."

As they sat in that dimly lit booth, the sounds of the bar fading into the background. The two continued to discuss particulars how they would make the most impact with the least amount of detriment to endangering themselves or others. This included their loved ones. Robert thought of how lucky he was that SuJin had not been physically harmed by the Russian and Korean mobs. For a moment he felt like the woman at the bar was listening in to their conversation. He looked over Daniel's shoulder to the young woman, who appeared consumed by her drink. Turning back to Daniel, he placed all his attention on the conversation.

Daniel knew his life had just taken an irrevocable turn. It felt as if he was on the most dangerous rollercoaster, and he could not get off. Things were happening so fast, he thought, and what if he were to do something irreversible. What if someone were hurt, or worst yet, killed? What if he was sent to prison? All these negative thoughts rushed through his mind, with no clear resolution other than he needed to at least be able to protect himself. The night stretched out before them, full of danger and possibility. Whatever came next, he was ready to face it head-on.

Chapter 7
Training Day

The sun crept over the horizon, painting the mountainside in hues of gold and amber. A gentle breeze rustled through the trees, carrying with it the crisp scent of pine and the promise of a new day. In a small clearing, nestled between ancient trees and weathered boulders, two figures moved with purpose and intensity. Daniel and Robert had been at it since before dawn, their bodies glistening with sweat despite the cool morning air. This secluded spot, far from the prying eyes of Seoul's bustling streets, had become their sanctuary, their training ground.

Robert's voice cut through the air, sharp and commanding. "Again!" he barked, as Daniel picked himself up from the ground for what felt like the hundredth time.

Daniel gritted his teeth, ignoring the protest of his aching muscles as he assumed a fighting stance. Robert came at him again, a flurry of precise strikes that Daniel struggled to block. But this time, something clicked. Daniel saw an opening and took it, his fist connecting solidly with Robert's ribs.

Robert grunted, a glimmer of pride in his eyes as he stepped back. "Better," he said, nodding approvingly. "You're starting to see the patterns."

As the sun climbed higher, their training intensified. They moved from hand-to-hand combat to weapons training, Robert demonstrating the proper technique for wielding a simple wooden staff. Daniel watched intently, his brow furrowed in concentration as he mimicked the movements.

"Remember," Robert said, his voice stern but not unkind, "the weapon is an extension of your body. Feel its weight, its balance. Let it become a part of you."

Hours passed in a blur of activity. They practiced throws and grapples, learning how to use an opponent's strength against them. They honed their skills with throwing knives, the thud of steel embedding in wood echoing through the clearing. As the sun reached its zenith, Robert called for a break. They sat cross-legged in the center of the clearing, their eyes closed in meditation. The sounds of the forest faded away as they focused on their breathing, centering themselves.

"The mind is your greatest weapon," Robert's voice came softly, barely above a whisper. "Train it as diligently as you train your body."

In the afternoon, they moved to strength training. Improvised weights made from rocks and logs tested their endurance. Daniel's muscles screamed in protest, but he pushed through, Robert's encouraging words spurring him on.

As the day waned, they faced off against imaginary groups of attackers. Robert taught Daniel how to move, how to position himself to avoid being surrounded. "Always be aware of your surroundings," he instructed. "Use the environment to your advantage."

Finally, as the sun began to dip below the treeline, Robert called an end to the day's training. Daniel collapsed onto the grass, his body aching but his spirit soaring. He felt stronger, more capable than he ever had before.

Robert sat down beside him, his own exhaustion evident but a look of satisfaction on his face. "You did well today," he said, his tone softer than it had been all day. "You're learning quickly."

Daniel turned to look at his mentor, curiosity burning in his eyes. "Robert," he began, hesitating for a moment before plunging ahead, "where did you learn all this?"

A shadow passed over Robert's face, a flicker of something - pain? regret? - in his eyes. But it was gone as quickly as it had appeared. "That's a story for another time," he said, his voice firm. "For now, focus on what's ahead. We have a long way to go, and the real challenge is yet to come."

As they gathered their things and prepared to head back to the city, Daniel couldn't shake the feeling that he was on the cusp of something monumental. The skills he was learning, the strength he was building - it all felt like preparation for a storm that was gathering on the horizon. The sun set behind them as they made their way down the mountain, casting long shadows ahead. Whatever lay in store for them in the depths of Seoul's underworld, Daniel knew one thing for certain - he would be ready to face it head-on.

The rhythmic thud of fists against leather echoed through the dimly lit gym. Sweat dripped from Daniel's brow, his breath coming in controlled, measured gasps as he unleashed a flurry of punches against the heavy bag. This local gym, tucked away in a basement beneath a nondescript building in Seoul, had become Daniel's second home. The peeling paint on the walls, the faint smell of sweat and disinfectant, the soft grunts of other patrons pushing their limits - it all faded into the background as Daniel focused on his training.

Thud. Thud. Thud.

Each impact sent a jolt up his arm, but Daniel welcomed the sensation. It was a reminder of how far he'd come, of the strength he was building. He could still hear Robert's voice in his head, guiding him even when his mentor wasn't present. "Keep your guard up," the phantom Robert instructed. "Don't telegraph your moves."

Daniel adjusted his stance, tightening his core as he transitioned from punches to kicks. His leg whipped out, connecting with the bag with a satisfying smack. Again and again, he repeated the motion, each kick more powerful than the last. As he trained, Daniel's mind wandered to the streets above. Somewhere out there, the Russian mafia was making their moves. The Jopok were plotting their next steps. And caught in the middle were countless innocent lives, people like SuJin, unaware of the dangers lurking in the shadows. The thought fueled his efforts. Daniel attacked the bag with renewed vigor, his movements becoming sharper, more precise. He was no longer just going through the motions; each strike was imbued with purpose, with the determination to make a difference.

Time seemed to blur as Daniel lost himself in the rhythm of his training. Punch, kick, dodge, weave. The bag swayed under his onslaught, chains creaking in protest. Other gym-goers cast curious glances his way, some nodding in approval at his intensity. Finally, exhaustion began to set in. Daniel's movements slowed, his breaths becoming more labored. With one final, powerful roundhouse kick, he stepped back from the bag, chest heaving. As he unwrapped his hands, Daniel caught sight of his reflection in a nearby mirror. The man staring back at him was a far cry from the naive foreigner who had first arrived in Seoul. His eyes held a newfound intensity, his posture speaking of hard-earned strength and confidence.

But with that strength came responsibility. Daniel knew that the skills he was honing weren't just for show. Soon, he would be putting them to the test against real opponents, with real stakes. As he gathered his things and prepared to leave the gym, Daniel felt a mix of anticipation and apprehension. The city above was a battlefield, and he was preparing to step into the fray. But for the first time since this all began, he felt ready - ready to face whatever challenges lay ahead, ready to make a stand against the darkness that threatened to engulf Seoul. With one last look at the battered punching bag, Daniel headed for the exit. The real fight was yet to come, but here, in this humble gym, he had laid the groundwork for victory. Whatever tomorrow might bring, Daniel knew one thing for certain - he would face it head-on, with everything he had.

Sunlight filtered through the traditional paper windows of Robert's home, casting a warm glow over the low table where he sat. The room was a study in contrasts - ancient wooden beams overhead, a state-of-the-art laptop humming quietly in the corner, and scattered across every surface, sheets of paper covered in intricate designs. Robert's hand moved with practiced precision across the page, his pencil bringing to life the vision in his mind. The scratching of graphite on paper was the only sound in the room, a rhythmic counterpoint to his measured breathing. On the page before him, a figure began to take shape. Sleek lines formed a costume that spoke of both stealth and strength. The dominant colors were black and red - black for the shadows they would move in, red for the passion and danger of their mission. Robert's eyes narrowed as he added details - reinforced panels for protection, hidden pockets for equipment, a mask that would conceal identity while allowing for clear vision.

As he worked, Robert's mind wandered to Daniel, to the progress his protégé had made. The costume wasn't just a flight of fancy - it was a necessity for what lay ahead. They needed to become more than men; they needed to become symbols. Setting aside the costume design, Robert turned his attention to a fresh sheet. Here, with swift, sure strokes, he began to sketch a logo. The shape of a chess knight emerged, viewed in profile. It was a fitting symbol, Robert mused - the knight, capable of unorthodox moves, jumping over obstacles, a piece that could turn the tide of a game when used skillfully. The logo was more than just a visual identifier. It was a statement of intent, a promise to the city they aimed to protect. Like knights of old, they would stand against the darkness, championing those who couldn't defend themselves.

As the day wore on, Robert's table became covered with variations of the costume and logo. Some were discarded, crumpled balls of paper testament to paths not taken. Others were refined, each iteration bringing the design closer to perfection. Finally, as the sun began to dip towards the horizon, Robert sat back, surveying his work. The final design lay before him - a costume that balanced functionality with symbolism, and a logo that would strike fear into the hearts of their enemies and inspire hope in those they protected.

Robert allowed himself a small smile of satisfaction. This was more than just artwork; it was the birth of something greater. With these designs, he and Daniel would transform from mere vigilantes into something more - guardians of Seoul, shadows that moved in the night to right the wrongs that the law couldn't touch. As he carefully gathered the designs, Robert's mind turned to the next steps. There would be materials to source, modifications to make, skills to hone. But looking at the knight logo staring up at him from the page, he felt a surge of determination. They were on the right path. The sun set over Seoul, painting the sky in shades of red that matched Robert's designs. In the gathering darkness, he could almost see their future taking shape - two figures, clad in black and red, moving through the night to bring justice to a city in need. The game was changing, and with these designs, Robert had just introduced a powerful new piece to the board.

Chapter 8
The First Mission

The abandoned warehouse on the outskirts of Seoul stood silent, its corrugated metal walls keeping the city's prying eyes at bay. Inside, the cavernous space echoed with purpose as Robert and Daniel prepared for their first mission as the Knight Squad. Fluorescent lights flickered to life, illuminating a makeshift command center. Tables laden with equipment lined the walls, each item meticulously chosen and placed. The air thrummed with tension and excitement. Robert moved with practiced efficiency, his hands sure as he began to don the uniform he had so carefully designed. The black fabric, reinforced with cutting-edge materials, seemed to absorb the light around it. He pulled on the pants, feeling the familiar weight of hidden armor plates. Across the room, Daniel mirrored his actions. His movements were less fluid than Robert's, but filled with a determined energy. He zipped up the jacket, marveling at how it fit like a second skin, allowing for full range of motion while offering crucial protection.

Robert secured a utility belt around his waist, each pouch filled with specialized gear. Daniel strapped on reinforced boots, testing their grip on the concrete floor. After pulling on his gloves Daniel noticed how they felt, flexible yet strong, designed for both combat and delicate operations. As they worked, the transformation was palpable. With each piece of equipment, each layer of the uniform, Robert and Daniel shed their civilian identities. In their place, the Knights were emerging - guardians ready to take on the darkness that plagued their city. Robert paused, holding up the final piece of the uniform - the mask. Its sleek design incorporated advanced filtration technology. But more than that, it was the symbol of their new identities. He met Daniel's eyes across the room, sensing his protégé's mix of nervousness and determination.

"Remember," Robert said, his voice low and steady, "once we put these on, there's no going back. We're no longer just Robert and Daniel. We become something more - something the city needs."

Daniel nodded, his jaw set with resolve. "I'm ready," he replied, his voice firm.

In unison, they donned the masks. The warehouse seemed to hold its breath as the transformation completed. Where two men had stood moments before, now two Knights rose - figures of shadow and purpose, ready to bring justice to the streets of Seoul.

Robert turned to the far wall, where their emblem - the chess knight in profile - had been painted in bold red strokes. It seemed to pulse with energy in the dim light, a beacon of their mission. "Let's move," Robert said, his voice slightly muffled by the mask but losing none of its authority.

As they made their final equipment checks, the air crackled with anticipation. The Knights were ready for their first sortie, prepared to step into the night and challenge the forces that had long held Seoul in their grip. The warehouse door slid open, revealing the fading light of day. Without a backward glance, the two figures slipped into the gathering dusk, melding with the shadows. The Knight Squad had been born, and Seoul would never be the same.

The night air hung heavy in the narrow alleyway, thick with the steam rising from vents and the acrid scent of the city's underbelly. Neon signs cast an eerie, ever-shifting glow, their garish colors reflecting off puddles and illuminating the mist in otherworldly hues. Flickering lamps struggled against the encroaching darkness, creating a dance of shadows along the graffiti-covered walls. Into this urban twilight zone stepped two figures that seemed born of the night itself. Knightmaire and Demon Knight moved with deliberate grace, their black and red uniforms melding seamlessly with the play of light and shadow. Steam swirled around their feet, parting like a curtain as they advanced.

Knightmaire, once known as Robert, led the way. His posture was alert, head swiveling slowly as he scanned their surroundings. The mask that obscured his features gleamed dully in the neon light, its eyepieces reflecting the kaleidoscope of colors around them. Every movement was measured, every step silent despite the litter-strewn ground. Behind him, Demon Knight - Daniel's alter ego - followed closely. His movements mirrored Knightmaire's, but with an underlying tension that spoke of barely contained energy. Where Knightmaire was the embodiment of calm vigilance, Demon Knight radiated a fierce readiness for action. As they progressed deeper into the alley, the sounds of the city seemed to fade away. The distant wail of sirens, the bass thump of music from hidden clubs, the occasional shout or laugh - all muted, as if the alley existed in a world apart from the Seoul they knew.

Their pace was unhurried, yet purposeful. This was more than a patrol; it was a statement. With each step, they were claiming this forgotten corner of the city, serving notice to the shadows that new guardians had arisen. A stray cat yowled and darted away, startled by their approach. Demon Knight's hand twitched towards a concealed weapon, but a subtle gesture from Knightmaire stayed his motion. This was not the threat they were here to face. As they neared the end of the alley, where it opened onto a wider street, Knightmaire paused. He turned to Demon Knight, the red accents of his uniform catching the light like fresh blood.

"Remember," Knightmaire's voice was low, distorted slightly by his mask, "we're not here to seek out conflict. We observe, we learn, and we intervene only when necessary. The city needs to know we exist, but it's not time to show our full hand yet."

Demon Knight nodded, his posture straightening with resolve. "Understood," he replied, his own voice carrying a hint of eagerness despite the modulation of his mask. With a final shared look, a moment of silent communication born from months of training together, they stepped out of the alley and into the bustling street beyond. The Knight Squad had made their first appearance, a glimpse of shadow and purpose in a city teetering on the brink of chaos. As they melded into the crowd, moving with the fluid grace of predators among prey, the message was clear. A new force had awakened in Seoul, and the balance of power was about to shift.

The cool night air whipped around Knightmaire and Demon Knight as they stood atop the weathered concrete of the rooftop. Below them, Seoul's nightlife pulsed with frenetic energy, a river of neon and shadow. Their gaze, however, was fixed on a single point amidst the chaos - the Russian bar, its gaudy Cyrillic sign a beacon in the night. Knightmaire's posture was statue-like. Beside him, Demon Knight shifted his weight from foot to foot, barely containing his eagerness for action.

"Patience," Knightmaire murmured, his voice low but carrying easily to his partner's ears. "We wait, we watch, we learn."

As if on cue, movement at the bar's entrance caught their attention. A figure emerged, his expensive suit and cautious demeanor marking him as someone of importance. Even from their vantage point, they could see the telltale bulge of a concealed weapon beneath his jacket. "Sasha Romanov," Knightmaire identified the man, a note of grim satisfaction in his voice. "Mid-level enforcer for the Russian outfit. Known for his brutality, but not his brains."

Demon Knight tensed, his hand instinctively moving towards his utility belt. "Are we going to move on him?"

Knightmaire held up a hand, staying his partner's eagerness. "Not yet. Let's see where he leads us."

Below, oblivious to the watchful eyes above, Sasha Romanov glanced furtively up and down the street before turning sharply into a narrow alley. His furtive movements spoke volumes - whatever business he was on, it wasn't sanctioned by his superiors. "Now," Knightmaire said, his voice hardening with resolve. "We move."

In perfect synchronization, born from months of rigorous training, Knightmaire and Demon Knight sprang into action. They moved with fluid grace to the edge of the rooftop, pulling out grappling guns in one smooth motion. With a soft pneumatic hiss, their grappling hooks shot out, finding purchase on a neighboring building. For a heartbeat, they stood poised on the precipice, the city spread out beneath them like a glittering tapestry.

Then, they were airborne. The wind rushed past as they descended. They landed in the alley with barely a sound, the advanced materials of their suits absorbing the impact. Knightmaire gestured silently, and Demon Knight nodded in understanding. They split up, moving down opposite sides of the alley, keeping to the deepest shadows. Ahead, Sasha Romanov's footsteps echoed off the grimy walls, leading them deeper into the labyrinth of Seoul's back streets. As they pursued their quarry, the air seemed to thicken with anticipation. This was more than just a chase - it was the beginning of their crusade against the corruption that plagued their city. With each step, Knightmaire and Demon Knight were writing the opening chapter of their legend.

The Knight Squad was on the move, and the underworld of Seoul was about to learn that the rules of the game had changed. The hunters had become the hunted, and justice was closing in. The night air hung heavy in the narrow alleyway, thick with steam that rose from grates in the pavement. Neon signs cast an eerie glow, their garish colors reflecting off puddles and mixing with the sickly yellow light of flickering lamps. The effect was disorienting, shadows shifting and dancing in the uneven illumination. Sasha strode into the alley, his footsteps echoing off the damp brick walls. He walked with purpose, completely unaware of the danger that lurked in the darkness behind him. Two figures detached themselves from the shadows, moving with practiced stealth as they closed in on their unsuspecting prey.

Knightmaire, a looming presence in black tactical gear, nodded silently to his partner. Demon Knight, a wiry man with a face hidden behind an ornate mask, slipped forward. In a heartbeat, he was on Sasha. The first blow caught Sasha completely off guard, sending him staggering. Adrenaline surged through his body as he spun to face his attacker. Demon Knight was already pressing his advantage, a flurry of strikes forcing Sasha onto the defensive. Sasha's mind raced as he frantically tried to fend off the assault. He managed to block a punch, countering with a wild swing that Demon Knight easily evaded. The fight was brutal but brief, a whirlwind of fists and desperate grappling. Despite his best efforts, Sasha found himself outmatched and overwhelmed.

Exhausted and battered, Sasha slumped against the alley wall. His chest heaved as he raised his hands in surrender, eyes darting between his two assailants. Knightmaire stepped forward, his massive frame dwarfing Sasha. With a speed that belied his size, he grabbed Sasha by the collar and slammed him back

92

against the bricks. Sasha's feet dangled, toes barely scraping the ground as Knightmaire lifted him effortlessly.

Knightmaire's eyes burned with cold fury behind his mask. When he spoke, his voice was a menacing growl that sent chills down Sasha's spine. "Tell your friends that the police aren't the only ones who are watching you."

The threat hung in the air, punctuated by the distant wail of sirens and the steady drip of water from a rusted pipe overhead. Sasha swallowed hard, the taste of blood and fear bitter on his tongue as he realized just how deep he'd gotten himself into this mess.

Sasha's mind reeled, terror and confusion etched across his face. He struggled to form words, his English failing him in this moment of extreme stress. "I... I don't understand what you say," he stammered, the words coming out in a thick accent.

Knightmaire turned to Demon Knight, his eyes narrowing behind his mask. Even without seeing his full expression, the sarcasm in his glare was palpable. Demon Knight responded with a slight, sinister smile, a silent communication passing between the two assailants.

With deliberate slowness, Demon Knight moved closer to Sasha. The fluorescent lights glinted off his mask, distorting his features into something almost inhuman.

When he spoke, his voice was low and menacing, each word dripping with threat. "You'll understand this..."

In one fluid motion, Demon Knight produced a small object from his pocket and tossed it at Sasha's feet. It clattered on the wet pavement, a chess piece - a knight - its surface a deep, unsettling crimson.

Sasha's hands trembled as he bent to pick up the piece. As his fingers closed around it, he felt something wet and sticky. He raised it to eye level, his breath catching in his throat as he saw the red smears now staining his skin. "Is this blood?" Sasha whispered, his voice barely audible over the ambient noise of the city.

Knightmaire suddenly released his grip on Sasha's collar, causing him to stumble. Without a backward glance, the imposing figure began to walk away, his heavy boots splashing through shallow puddles. His parting words hung in the air like a death sentence. "It'll be your blood if you don't leave town tonight."

Sasha watched, frozen in place, as the two mysterious attackers melted back into the shadows of the alley. His heart pounded in his chest, the bloody chess piece clutched tightly in his fist. As the reality of the threat sank in, Sasha realized that his life in this city had just become a dangerous game - one where he was nothing more than a pawn caught between powerful, ruthless players. With shaking legs, he pushed himself off the wall and began to run, desperate to put as much distance as possible between himself and this nightmarish encounter. The neon lights blurred as he fled, the knight piece a damning weight in his pocket, leaving him with an impossible choice: flee or face consequences he could scarcely imagine. As quickly as they had appeared, Knightmaire and Demon Knight vanished into the night. The steam from the grates seemed to thicken, swirling around their retreating forms until they were swallowed by the darkness. One moment they were there, menacing presences dominating the alley, and the next they were gone - leaving only fear and uncertainty in their wake.

Sasha's legs gave out beneath him. He collapsed to his knees on the cold, damp pavement, his body shaking uncontrollably. The adrenaline that had sustained him during the confrontation was fading, replaced by waves of pain from the beating he'd endured. He looked down at his trembling hands, still clutching the blood-red knight piece. A drop of blood - his own blood - fell from a cut on his lip, landing on the chess piece. The fresh crimson mingled with the dried stains, a chilling reminder of the threat that now hung over him. Sasha's eyes darted frantically around the alley, searching for any sign of his attackers, but he found himself utterly alone in the neon-lit gloom. His fingers closed tightly around the knight piece, its edges digging into his palm. With a sudden burst of desperate energy, Sasha scrambled to his feet. He stumbled at first, nearly losing his balance, before finding his footing. Without a backward glance, he fled down the alley, his footsteps echoing off the walls as he ran from the scene of his terrifying encounter.

Unknown to Sasha, he wasn't as alone as he thought. From a vantage point high above the alley, a solitary figure watched the drama unfold. Han stood motionless in the shadows of a fire escape, his keen eyes taking in every detail of the confrontation below. He observed the Knight Squad's methods with professional interest, noting their efficiency and the fear they instilled in their target. As Sasha disappeared around a corner, Han's gaze shifted to the spot where Knightmaire and Demon Knight had vanished. His expression remained impassive, but his mind raced with the implications of what he'd witnessed. This was a new player in the game, a wild card that could upset the delicate balance of power in the city's underworld. Han melted back into the darkness, moving with the silent grace of a seasoned operative. He had information to report, plans to adjust. The night's events had changed the playing field, and Han intended to ensure he and his allies were prepared for whatever came next. In the streets below, the city continued its nocturnal rhythm, oblivious to the deadly chess match that had just made its opening move in that steam-filled alley.

Chapter 9
Nicholi's Frustration

The cool night air whipped across the rooftop, carrying with it the distant sounds of the city below. Knightmaire and Demon Knight emerged from the shadows, their movements fluid and purposeful as they crossed the gravel-strewn surface. The adrenaline of their recent confrontation still coursed through their veins, lending an electric energy to their postures.

Knightmaire's hand shot out suddenly, grabbing Demon Knight by the shoulder and pulling him aside. The larger man's grip was firm, a silent reminder of his authority. When he spoke, his voice was low and tense, barely audible over the ambient noise of traffic far below. "What was that with the toy?"

Demon Knight's eyes flickered down to where Knightmaire's gloved hand gripped his uniform. There was a moment of tension between them, the air thick with unspoken challenge. When Demon Knight responded, his tone was carefully neutral, walking a fine line between explanation and defiance. "Okay, man," he said, emphasizing the casual address. "I just considered it a calling card."

Knightmaire held his partner's gaze for a long moment, his expression unreadable behind his mask. Then, with deliberate slowness, he released his grip on Demon Knight's uniform. The fabric, bunched under his fingers, slowly smoothed out as he withdrew his hand.

"Let me know before you do something like that again," Knightmaire growled, his words carrying the weight of an order rather than a request.

The two stood facing each other, the city skyline a glittering backdrop to their tense exchange. The partnership between them was clearly a complex one, built on a foundation of shared purpose but not without its friction points. Demon Knight's improvisation had crossed a line, however fine, in Knightmaire's eyes. As they stood there on the rooftop, the cool breeze carrying the scent of the city, it was clear that this was more than just a reprimand. It was a moment that defined the dynamics of their relationship, a subtle power play that would shape their future interactions.

The sounds of sirens in the distance broke the moment, a reminder of the larger game they were playing. Without another word, both men turned their attention back to the city sprawled out before them, united once again in their shadowy purpose.

The neon sign of the Russian club flickered erratically, casting an unsteady red glow over the rain-slicked street. The Cyrillic letters buzzed and hummed, a beacon in the night for those seeking a taste of home in this foreign city. Sasha emerged from the shadows, his gait uneven and pained. Each step sent a jolt of agony through his body, a stark reminder of the beating he'd endured in the alley. His clothes were disheveled, dark stains - some from the damp alley floor, others unmistakably blood - marred the fabric.

As he approached the club's entrance, Sasha's hand instinctively went to his pocket, fingers closing around the blood-stained chess piece. The weight of it, so small yet so significant, seemed to pull him down, making each step more laborious than the last. The throbbing bass of Russian pop music spilled out onto the street each time the door opened, along with raucous laughter and the acrid smell of cigarette smoke.

Sasha paused for a moment, gathering what little strength he had left. His mind raced with the implications of the night's events, knowing that stepping through that door meant involving others in his dangerous situation. With a deep breath that sent pain lancing through his ribs, Sasha steeled himself and pushed forward. He limped past the stern-faced bouncer, who gave him a concerned look but said nothing. In this neighborhood, it wasn't uncommon for patrons to arrive looking worse for wear.

As Sasha disappeared into the smoky interior of the club, the street outside fell quiet once more. The neon sign continued its erratic dance, oblivious to the drama unfolding within its walls, where a man with a bloodied chess piece was about to change the course of many lives. The interior of the Russian club was a haze of cigarette smoke and dim lighting, the air thick with the scent of vodka and nostalgia.

In a secluded booth at the far end, Nicholi reclined like a king holding court. His expensive suit stood out among the working-class patrons, a silent testament to his status. A half-smoked cigar dangled from his fingers as he conversed in low tones with two burly men - his ever-present henchmen. The relative calm of their conversation was shattered as Sasha stumbled through the crowd, his labored breathing audible even over the pulsing music. Heads turned to watch his desperate progress across the room, whispers and concerned glances following in his wake.

"Boss... boss!" Sasha gasped as he reached Nicholi's table, his voice ragged with pain and urgency. "We got problems!"

Nicholi's gaze swept over Sasha's battered form, taking in the bruises, the torn clothing, the wild look in his eyes. His expression hardened, a mixture of disgust and disappointment evident in the curl of his lip.

"What... are you talking about?" Nicholi's voice was cold, each word carefully measured.

Unable to stand any longer, Sasha collapsed to his knees beside the table. With trembling hands, he reached into his pocket and produced the blood-stained chess piece, holding it up like a supplicant presenting an offering.

"I was attacked by some locals or something," Sasha babbled, his words tumbling out in a frantic rush. "They threatened all of us to get out of Korea, and handed me this!"

The club seemed to fall silent around them, the weight of Sasha's words hanging heavy in the air. Nicholi leaned forward slightly, his eyes fixed on the crimson-stained knight. His hand, adorned with heavy gold rings, twitched as if to reach for it, but he held back.

"Is that your blood?" Nicholi asked, his tone deceptively casual.

Sasha glanced down at the chess piece, then at his own bloodied hands, as if seeing them for the first time. The realization seemed to hit him anew, the full impact of the night's events crashing over him in a wave of fear and pain. Nicholi's eyes narrowed as he studied Sasha's reaction. The wheels were already turning in his mind, calculating the implications of this unexpected threat.

Around them, the other patrons pretended not to watch, but there was no mistaking the tension that had suddenly gripped the room.

In that moment, as Sasha knelt bleeding on the floor of a Russian club in Korea, clutching a blood-stained chess piece, it was clear that a dangerous new game had begun. And Nicholi, whether he liked it or not, had just been dealt in. Nicholi's eyes never left the chess piece as he raised a hand, fingers snapping in a sharp gesture. Natasha, a striking woman who had been observing silently from the edge of the booth, stepped forward immediately. Her movements were fluid and precise as she bent down, plucking the bloodied knight from Sasha's trembling fingers. With delicate care that belied the grim nature of the object, Natasha placed the chess piece on the table in front of Nicholi. The red-stained ivory stood out starkly against the dark wood, a silent harbinger of the trouble that had found them. Nicholi let his guard down, watching Natasha as she strutted away. But only for a moment, as he remembered that he needed to retain his fierce demeanor as the tough and terrifying leader of this group. Nicholi stiffened his face, reestablishing a tense and striking stare back in Sasha's direction.

Once Nicholi's demeanor shifted, his casual posture giving way to a taut alertness, he felt that he could return to the business at hand. His gaze snapped to the far corner of the bar where a group of men sat, their attentive postures marking them as more than mere patrons. With another sharp snap of his fingers, Nicholi
102

called out in rapid-fire Russian, his voice low but carrying an unmistakable edge of command. "Get out there and find these thugs!"

The men rose as one, their movements synchronized and purposeful. They filed out of the club without a word, the crowd parting instinctively to let them pass. The air in the club grew even tenser, the other patrons now acutely aware that something significant was unfolding.

Nicholi turned his attention back to Sasha, who still knelt on the floor, looking more wretched by the moment. When Nicholi spoke again, his voice was calmer, but there was steel beneath the surface. "Sasha, I want you to tell me exactly what happened... from the beginning."

Sasha swallowed hard, his Adam's apple bobbing visibly. He pulled himself up, wincing as he slid into the booth across from Nicholi. The henchmen shifted to make room, their faces impassive but their eyes alert, watching Sasha's every move. As Sasha began to recount his harrowing encounter in the alley, Nicholi leaned back, his fingers steepled in front of him. His eyes never left Sasha's face, scrutinizing every detail, every flicker of emotion.

The chess piece sat between them on the table, a silent reminder of the threat they now faced. As Sasha's tale unfolded, it became clear that the peaceful facade of their operations in Korea had been shattered. A new player had entered the game, and Nicholi's expression grew darker with each word, the implications of this bold move against his people sinking in.

The Russian club, once a haven of familiarity in a foreign land, now felt like a war room. Plans would need to be made, alliances tested, and retribution dealt. As Sasha's story reached its climax, Nicholi's mind was already racing ahead, plotting their next move in this unexpected and dangerous game.

Chapter 10
Han the Informant

The fluorescent lights of the subway car flickered intermittently, casting an artificial glow over the sparse interior. Daniel stood in the center of the car, his posture a stark contrast to his usual demeanor. Gone was the hunched, uncertain stance of a man trying to disappear into the background. In its place was something new - a figure radiating quiet confidence and heightened awareness. His eyes, once downcast and avoiding contact, now scanned the empty car with purpose. Every movement, every slight change in the subway's motion, seemed to register in his alert gaze. It was as if he were seeing his surroundings for the first time, truly conscious of the space he occupied. Daniel's attention drifted down to his hands.

His knuckles were swollen and discolored, vivid purples and yellows painting a canvas of recent violence across his skin. Instead of wincing at the sight or hiding the evidence of conflict, a small smile played at the corners of his mouth. He flexed his fingers slowly, feeling the dull ache of bruised flesh and bone. Each throb of pain seemed to affirm something for him, a physical reminder of a transformation taking place within. The smile on his face deepened, not one of joy but of grim satisfaction.

Daniel stood tall, a man changed. The bruises on his fists told a story of confrontation, of crossing a line he'd never dared approach before. And judging by the set of his shoulders and the glint in his eye, it was clear this was only the beginning. The driverless car sped on, carrying Daniel towards whatever awaited him at the next station. But it was evident that the man who would step off this train was fundamentally different from the one who had boarded it in the past. The city that had once intimidated him might soon find itself facing a new force to be reckoned with.

The Korean National Museum stood majestic in the night, its grand architecture illuminated by strategically placed lights that cast long shadows across the grounds. The air was crisp, carrying with it the faint scent of blooming flowers from the nearby gardens. Daniel approached the museum with purpose, his stride confident and measured. Movement in his peripheral vision caught his attention. His head snapped around, eyes narrowing as he recognized a
106

familiar figure in the distance – Jessica. Without hesitation, Daniel quickened his pace, weaving between the sparse crowd of late-night visitors. His heart raced, not from exertion but from the sudden surge of adrenaline that coursed through him at the sight of her. Jessica walked along the far end of the front entrance, her silhouette graceful against the backdrop of the museum's façade. Suddenly, she paused mid-step. Her head tilted down slightly, as if listening to some unheard whisper. In that moment, it seemed as though she sensed the weight of Daniel's gaze upon her.

With fluid grace, Jessica moved towards a massive pillar, disappearing behind its ornate surface. Daniel's breath caught in his throat as he closed the distance, anticipation building with each step. He reached the pillar, his hand outstretched to round its curve, only to be met with empty space. Jessica had vanished, leaving no trace of her presence. Daniel's eyes darted around, searching the surrounding area for any sign of her, but finding nothing. A buzzing sensation against his leg broke his concentration. Frustration etched across his features as he pulled out his cell phone. The screen lit up with a notification – Robert was trying to reach him.

Daniel stared at the phone for a long moment, conflict evident in the set of his jaw. He looked up once more, scanning the museum grounds in a final, futile attempt to spot Jessica. With a resigned shrug that spoke volumes about his inner turmoil, Daniel turned away from the pillar. The weight of the missed encounter and the looming conversation with Robert seemed to press down on his shoulders. The night that had started with such promise now felt tinged with disappointment and unresolved tension.

Daniel disappeared into the night, leaving behind the silent pillars of the museum – and the lingering mystery of Jessica's vanishing act. The encounter, brief as it was, had stirred something within him, adding another layer of complexity to the evolving tapestry of his life. Jessica emerged from her hiding place. She moved with calculated grace, her eyes never leaving Daniel's retreating form until he vanished from sight. A mixture of emotions played across her face - relief, regret, and something deeper, more complex.

With a quick glance around to ensure she wasn't observed, Jessica slipped behind the museum building. The shadows here were deeper, the silence more pronounced. She allowed herself a moment to collect her thoughts, her back pressed against the cool stone of the structure. Suddenly, a hand shot out from the darkness, grasping her arm. Jessica's body tensed, ready to defend herself, but recognition dawned as she looked up at the mysterious figure looming over her.

"You lied to me," Jessica hissed, her voice low but charged with anger and betrayal. "I did not know that it was him!"

The figure remained silent, their face obscured by the shadows. Jessica's words hung in the air between them, heavy with implication. It was clear that this encounter was part of a larger, more complicated scenario - one where Jessica had been kept in the dark about a crucial detail. The grip on her arm loosened slightly, but the tension in the air remained palpable. Jessica's eyes blazed with a mixture of fury and hurt, demanding answers from the silent figure before her. This moment of confrontation seemed to mark a turning point, a fracture in whatever alliance or arrangement had brought them to this clandestine meeting.

The night air grew colder around them, mirroring the chill that had settled between Jessica and her mysterious companion. Whatever plan had been set in motion, it was clear that Jessica was no longer a willing pawn - and the consequences of this revelation were bound to ripple through the intricate web of relationships and motivations that surrounded them.

Knightmaire stood at the edge of the rooftop, his imposing figure a darker silhouette against the urban landscape. His gaze swept methodically over the streets below, tracking movement and noting patterns with the practiced eye of a predator. Every few moments, Knightmaire's attention would flicker to the cell phone in his hand. The screen remained stubbornly dark, no messages appearing to break the monotony of his vigil. A tense energy radiated from him, his impatience for Demon Knight's arrival growing with each passing minute. The soft scrape of footsteps behind him broke the silence. In an instant, Knightmaire's body tensed, coiled and ready for action.

He spun around, weapon materializing in his hand as if conjured from the very shadows that cloaked him.

Han stood there, his approach having been nearly silent until the last moment. His hands were held up in a placating gesture, his posture deliberately non-threatening. When he spoke, his voice was calm, the words in Hangul carrying a hint of dry humor despite the tension of the moment. "Please do not attack me for intruding..."

Knightmaire's response was immediate and fluid. He dropped into a fighting stance, his weapon trained unerringly on Han's chest. The moonlight glinted off the barrel, a silent promise of lethal consequence. The two men stood frozen in this tableau, the sprawling city below oblivious to the drama unfolding high above its streets. Han's eyes, sharp and intelligent, studied Knightmaire, taking in every detail of his stance and equipment. Knightmaire, for his part, remained as still as a statue, only the slight rise and fall of his chest betraying that he was flesh and blood rather than stone. The air between them crackled with tension, a palpable force that seemed to distort the very night around them. This unexpected confrontation had the potential to explode into violence at any moment, or to reshape the landscape of alliances and enmities that defined their world.

Han's reaction was swift and calculated. His hands shot up higher, palms out, fingers spread wide - a universal gesture of surrender. Despite the threat of the weapon pointed at his chest, Han's voice remained steady. "Forgive me, but I only came to help."

Knightmaire's posture remained rigid, his weapon unwavering. His eyes, hidden behind his mask, swept over Han's form in a rapid, assessing gaze. He took in every detail - the cut of Han's clothes, the way he held himself, searching for any hint of concealed weapons or hostile intent.

When Knightmaire spoke, his voice was a low growl, the Hangul words carrying a clear note of warning despite the foreign tongue. "You need to leave now, old man."

The tension in the air seemed to thicken, the moment balanced on a knife's edge. Han, however, appeared unfazed by the threat. Slowly, deliberately, he lowered his arms. His body remained still, but there was a subtle shift in his demeanor - a quiet confidence that belied his apparent vulnerability. "You have been attacking those horrible Russians. I've seen you."

The words hung in the air between them, heavy with implication. Han's admission of knowledge was both a revelation and a gambit. He was laying his cards on the table, acknowledging his awareness of Knightmaire's activities while simultaneously aligning himself against a common enemy. Knightmaire's grip on his weapon tightened almost imperceptibly. The situation had suddenly become more complex. This wasn't just an intrusion to be dealt with; it was potentially a new player entering the game, one with unknown motives and allegiances. The next few moments would be crucial, determining whether Han would become an ally, an enemy, or a loose end to be tied up.

Knightmaire's posture shifted, his body language radiating a growing anger. The air around him seemed to crackle with tension, his patience clearly wearing thin. When he spoke again, he abandoned the pretense of using Hangul, his words coming out in crisp, threatening English. "I said leave now, or else."

The switch to English was deliberate, a power move designed to reassert control over the situation. But Han, it seemed, was not so easily intimidated. With slow, deliberate movements, he reached into his jacket pocket. Knightmaire's grip on his weapon tightened, ready to react at the slightest provocation.

Instead of a weapon, Han produced a small card. His voice remained calm as he spoke, still in Hangul, either unable or unwilling to match Knightmaire's linguistic shift. "Okay, I get it. I just thought you may want to know where the Russians will be later tonight."

With careful movements, Han bent down and placed the card on the ground in front of him. The white rectangle stood out starkly against the dark rooftop, a tantalizing piece of information just out of Knightmaire's reach. "I've been watching them also, and think they need to be removed from here altogether."

Han's words hung in the air, laden with implication. He was offering not just information, but alignment - a shared goal that could potentially bridge the gap between them. Without waiting for a response, Han turned and began to walk away, his movements unhurried and deliberate. Knightmaire was left alone on the rooftop, the city lights twinkling indifferently below. The card on the ground seemed to glow in the dim light, a beacon of possibility and potential danger. Knightmaire stood frozen, his mind racing. The unexpected encounter had thrown his carefully laid plans into disarray. Now, he faced a crucial decision: ignore the offered information and stick to the original plan, or adapt and potentially gain a valuable ally in their crusade against the Russians.

The tension on the rooftop was still palpable when Demon Knight emerged from the shadows. His arrival was silent, befitting his role, but his voice cut through the night air with an edge of anticipation. "I got your text. Are we doing this tonight?"

Knightmaire's reaction was subtle but telling. His gaze shifted past Demon Knight, scanning the area Han had just vacated. The unspoken question hung in the air: Had Demon Knight seen the mysterious visitor? Had their confrontation been witnessed? For a long moment, Knightmaire remained silent, his mind working through the implications of the unexpected encounter and the information Han had left behind. Finally, he turned his attention back to Demon Knight, his decision made.

"Yes, here's the place," Knightmaire said, his voice betraying no hint of the internal conflict he'd just resolved.

With a fluid motion, Knightmaire bent down and retrieved the card Han had left. He held it out to Demon Knight, the small rectangle of paper now a pivotal piece in their evolving strategy. Demon Knight reached for the card, the air between them seemed charged with unspoken questions. Knightmaire's decision not to mention Han's visit was deliberate, a calculated risk in their partnership. The information on the card could change everything, but its source would remain Knightmaire's secret, at least for now. Demon Knight studied the card, his expression hidden behind his mask but his body language speaking of focused intensity. As the two stood there, the weight of their impending action settling around them, it was clear that this night would mark a turning point. The Knights were about to make their move, armed with unexpected intelligence from an unknown player. The game was changing, and the stakes were higher than ever.

Chapter 11
Fighting the Russians

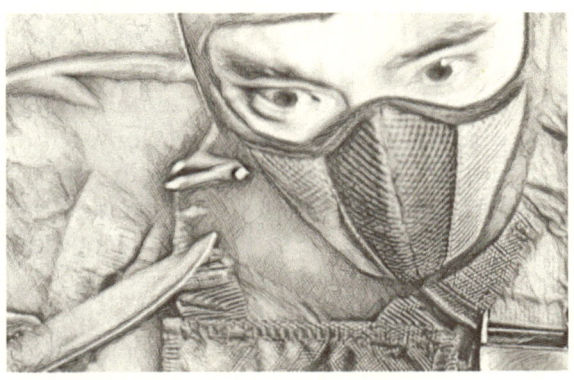

The night club pulsed with energy, a cacophony of thumping bass, flashing lights, and the indistinct chatter of patrons lost in their revelry. In a dimly lit corner booth, partially obscured by writhing bodies on the dance floor, sat Boris. His voice carried over the music, sharp and agitated as he barked orders and rifled through bags of drugs spread out before him like a twisted buffet. The air was thick with the scent of sweat, alcohol, and something more illicit. Boris's fingers moved deftly, weighing and packaging his wares with practiced efficiency. His eyes darted nervously around the club, a predator always on guard for potential threats or lucrative opportunities.

Suddenly, the atmosphere in the club shifted. It was subtle at first, a ripple of unease that spread through the crowd near the entrance. Then, like Moses parting the Red Sea, the mass of bodies began to separate, revealing a figure that seemed to absorb the pulsating lights rather than reflect them. Knightmaire stepped into the club, his presence a stark contrast to the revelry around him. His movements were deliberate, purposeful, each step bringing him closer to the Russian's stronghold. The music seemed to fade into the background, drowned out by the pounding of Boris's heart as he locked eyes with the masked intruder. Boris's hand froze mid-transaction, a bag of white powder suspended in the air. Recognition and fear flashed across his face in quick succession. He had heard whispers of masked vigilantes, but had dismissed them as urban legends. Now, faced with the reality, Boris felt a chill that had nothing to do with the club's air conditioning. Knightmaire's fists clenched at his sides, the leather of his gloves creaking audibly even in the noisy club. The message was clear: he hadn't come to dance.

With a sudden burst of movement, Boris stood up from the booth. His chair clattered to the floor, the sound lost in the thumping music but the motion drawing the attention of his associates. They turned, confusion giving way to alarm as they registered the threat. The club, oblivious to the brewing confrontation, continued its hedonistic rhythms. But in this corner, time seemed to stand still. Boris and Knightmaire faced each other across the crowded room, two forces poised on the brink of violent collision. The game was no longer about territory or profit margins. Tonight, in this

116

pulsating den of vice, justice had come calling, wearing a mask and carrying the promise of retribution. The tension in the club snapped like a rubber band stretched beyond its limit. In a blur of motion, Demon Knight emerged from the shadows, launching himself at Boris with predatory precision. The Russian barely had time to register the new threat before Demon Knight's fist connected with his jaw, sending him reeling back into the booth.

The fight erupted in a chaotic flurry of punches, kicks, and grapples. Boris, despite his surprise, was no stranger to violence. He fought back with the desperation of a cornered animal, his bulk and street-fighting experience momentarily keeping him in the game against Demon Knight's more refined techniques. Knightmaire stood impassive, observing the melee with clinical detachment. His stillness was a stark contrast to the violence unfolding before him, like the eye of a storm. Suddenly, movement from the back of the club caught Knightmaire's attention. Natasha burst through a door, her hands filled with glinting metal. Without hesitation, she unleashed a barrage of throwing knives, their blades singing through the air as they hurtled towards Knightmaire. With preternatural speed, Knightmaire twisted and weaved. The knives whistled past him, embedding themselves in the wall behind with dull thuds. In the space of a heartbeat, he closed the distance to Natasha.

The confrontation was brief and brutal. Natasha's expertise with blades counted for little in close quarters against Knightmaire's superior strength and skill. A flurry of strikes left Natasha dazed and stumbling. A final, decisive blow sent her crumpling to the floor, unconscious before she hit the ground. Meanwhile, Demon Knight had gained the upper hand against Boris. The Russian's initial fury had given way to fatigue, his movements growing sluggish and uncoordinated. With a final, crushing blow, Demon Knight sent Boris sprawling across the drug-laden table. As Boris lay groaning amidst the scattered packets of narcotics, Demon Knight reached into his jacket. He produced a chess piece – a knight, symbol of their crusade – and placed it deliberately on the table. The message was clear: the Knights had made their move in this deadly game.

With the immediate threats neutralized, Demon Knight turned and strode towards Knightmaire, who stood vigilant near the club's entrance. Around them, the few remaining patrons cowered in corners or fled in panic, the music now silent, replaced by the wail of approaching sirens.

The two Knights stood side by side, surveying the chaos they had wrought. In the span of minutes, they had dismantled a significant operation of the Russian underground. But both knew this was merely the opening gambit in a much larger conflict. As blue and red lights began to flash outside the club's windows, Knightmaire and Demon Knight exchanged a silent nod. Their work here was done, but the night was far from over. Without a word, they melted into the shadows, leaving behind a scene of destruction, a warning, and a mystery for the authorities to unravel.

As the chaos in the club settled into an eerie quiet, punctuated only by the distant wail of approaching sirens, Knightmaire turned to his partner. His voice was low, barely audible above the groans of the fallen Russians. "Did you recognize him?"

Demon Knight's gaze swept over the prone forms of Boris and Natasha. A slow nod of approval followed, the gesture speaking volumes about their shared history and the significance of this moment.

Knightmaire studied his partner closely, reading the subtle shifts in body language that betrayed Demon Knight's emotional state. "How did that feel?" he probed, his tone a mixture of curiosity and concern.

A smile spread across Demon Knight's face, visible even beneath his mask. It was a smile tinged with satisfaction, perhaps even a hint of dark pleasure. "Pretty good," he replied, his voice carrying a note of exhilaration.

The exchange was brief, but laden with meaning. It spoke of a shared mission, of personal vendettas intertwined with a broader sense of justice. The Knights had struck a significant blow against the Russian criminal element, but the victory seemed to carry a personal weight for Demon Knight. Without another word, Knightmaire and Demon Knight moved in perfect synchronization towards the exit. They navigated through the debris of their confrontation - overturned tables, scattered drugs, and the unconscious forms of their adversaries. The chess piece left behind glinted in the strobing lights, a calling card and a warning.

As they reached the door, the flashing lights of police vehicles became visible through the grimy windows. The Knights paused for a moment, silhouetted against the chaotic tableau they had created. Then, with practiced ease, they slipped into the shadows of the night. They vanished just as the first police officers burst through the door, leaving behind a scene of destruction, a dismantled drug operation, and a mystery that would soon set the city's underworld ablaze with rumor and fear. The Knights had made their move, and the game was irrevocably changed. As they melted into the darkness of the city streets, both Knightmaire and Demon Knight knew that this was only the beginning. The night was young, and their crusade was far from over.

The Russian club hummed with subdued activity, a stark contrast to its usual boisterous atmosphere. In a secluded booth at the far end, Nicholi reclined, a cloud of cigar smoke wreathing his head like a malevolent halo. His eyes, cold and calculating, were fixed on his companion, Deathstrike, whose massive frame was artfully concealed by the booth's arrangement.

Behind Nicholi, incongruous in its mundanity, sat a cardboard box. It was filled to the brim with chess pieces - knights, their once-pristine white now stained with varying shades of crimson. Each piece a silent testament to the growing threat facing their organization. The relative calm was shattered as Ivan stumbled into the club. His face was a canvas of bruises, his gait uneven and pained. He made a beeline for Nicholi's booth, desperation evident in every labored step.

As Ivan opened his mouth to speak, Nicholi raised a hand, silencing him with a gesture. His voice, when he spoke, was laden with a mixture of resignation and barely contained fury. The Russian words flowed smoothly, each sentence a prediction of Ivan's report. "Let me guess... you were attacked by some masked vigilantes."

Ivan's nod was a mixture of shame and confirmation. Nicholi continued, his tone growing colder with each word. "And you were unable to defeat them."

Another nod from Ivan, his eyes downcast. "And they gave you a bloody chess piece."

Ivan's final nod was accompanied by a trembling hand extending towards Nicholi, offering the damning evidence - another blood-stained knight to add to their growing collection. Nicholi took the piece, turning it over in his hands. His face remained impassive, but the tightening of his jaw and the flash in his eyes spoke volumes. This was no longer a minor irritation; it had become a full-blown crisis threatening their entire operation. The silence that fell over the booth was heavy with unspoken tensions and looming consequences. Ivan stood motionless, awaiting judgment, while Deathstrike remained a silent, ominous presence at Nicholi's side.

As Nicholi placed the new chess piece into the box with its brethren, the soft clink of ivory against ivory seemed to echo through the club. It was the sound of escalation, of a conflict spiraling towards an inevitable and violent conclusion. The game board was set, the pieces were in play, and Nicholi's next move would determine the fate of their criminal empire in this city. The Knights had made their presence known - now it was time for the Russians to respond. Nicholi examined the bloodstained chess piece for a moment, his face a mask of controlled fury. With a sudden, violent motion, he tossed it over his shoulder into the box behind him. The sound it made as it joined its fellows was telling - a loud clatter that spoke of numerous similar pieces already collected. Each one a mark of failure, a tally of humiliation.

Turning to Deathstrike, Nicholi switched to English, his words clipped and precise. "This is exactly what I was talking about. I do not like that I have to rely outside of my organization to clean up my problems, but it is time to step up our defenses."

With a sweep of his arm, Nicholi pulled the box onto the table. He upended it, spilling its contents across the polished surface. Dozens of knight pieces cascaded out, a macabre collection of ivory stained with varying shades of red. Some bore the dark brown of dried blood, others the brighter crimson of more recent encounters.

Nicholi's voice dropped to a menacing growl. "I want no more toys handed to me."

The words hung in the air, heavy with implication. This was no longer a nuisance to be tolerated, but a threat to be eliminated. At Nicholi's proclamation, Deathstrike rose from his seat. As he stood to his full height, the true enormity of his physique became apparent. He towered over the table, a mountain of muscle and barely contained violence. His presence seemed to suck the air out of the room, casting a shadow that dimmed the already low lights of the club.

Deathstrike's response was simple, but delivered with a quiet certainty that sent chills down the spines of all present. "Consider it done."

Without another word, he turned and began to walk away. As he moved past the gathered Russians, his massive frame seemed to fill the entire space. Each step was measured, purposeful, the floor seeming to tremble beneath his weight. Ivan, who had been standing nearby, looked up in awe and terror at Deathstrike's passing. He instinctively stepped back, pressing himself against the wall to make way. The contrast between Ivan's battered form and Deathstrike's imposing presence was stark - a vivid illustration of the escalation Nicholi had just set in motion.

As Deathstrike disappeared through the door, leaving a wake of stunned silence behind him, the atmosphere in the club shifted. There was a sense of grim anticipation, of a coming storm that would reshape the criminal landscape of the city. Nicholi turned back to the table, his eyes sweeping over the scattered chess pieces. Each one represented a failure, a humiliation. But now, they also represented a promise - a promise of retribution, of a counter-strike that would shake the very foundations of their unknown enemies. The Knights had made their move. Now, it was time for the Russians to unleash their own deadly game piece.

Chapter 12
Deathstrike

Sunlight streamed through the paper-screened windows of the traditional Korean home, casting a warm glow over the room where Daniel and Robert sat. The contrast between the ancient architecture and their modern vigilante discussion was stark, a reminder of the complex world they navigated.

Daniel leaned forward, his brow furrowed in thought. "Do you find it strange that we have not gone up against any Korean mafia yet?"

Robert's response was measured, his voice carrying a note of satisfaction. "We are doing a lot of good cleaning out the Russian elements."

"I know," Daniel conceded, his eyes distant as he processed their recent activities. "But it just strikes me as odd that the Koreans have been laying low through all of this."

Robert shrugged, a hint of a smile playing at the corners of his mouth. "Maybe they are smarter than to deal with us."

Daniel's unease was palpable, his words carrying a weight of foreboding. "I've got a bad feeling about this. Something isn't right."

Robert shifted, his posture becoming more businesslike. "Well, until we figure it out, we have another mission tonight. We're going to the market to shut down a counterfeiting ring."

At this, Daniel's eyes narrowed, a note of suspicion creeping into his voice. "Is this info fed from your local friend? Also a Korean?"

The question hung in the air between them, loaded with implications. Robert's connection to local sources had been invaluable, but Daniel's growing unease about the lack of confrontation with Korean criminal elements was casting those relationships in a new light.

The room fell silent, the peaceful ambiance of the traditional home at odds with the tension building between the two vigilantes. Outside, the sounds of daily life in Korea continued unabated, oblivious to the potential storm brewing within these walls.

Daniel and Robert held each other's gaze, years of partnership and trust now tinged with a hint of doubt. The complex dance of justice, loyalty, and cultural dynamics they had been performing was reaching a critical juncture.

As they sat there, surrounded by the trappings of Korean tradition, both men knew that their next moves would be crucial in unraveling the mystery that seemed to be enveloping their mission. The sunlight continued to pour in, illuminating the dust motes floating between them - silent witnesses to a partnership on the brink of a significant test.

Robert's voice took on a sharp edge, his eyes narrowing as he responded to Daniel's implied suspicion. "What's next, you think I'm part of your little conspiracy theory?"

The tension in the room ratcheted up a notch, years of trust and camaraderie suddenly on shaky ground. Daniel, realizing the impact of his words, backpedaled quickly, his tone softening with regret.

"No, sorry man," he said, running a hand through his hair in frustration. "It just feels too overwhelming... so much so quick, you know?"

The apology hung in the air between them, a fragile bridge over the chasm of doubt that had suddenly opened up. Robert's posture remained rigid, his jaw set as he considered Daniel's words. After a moment, he spoke, his voice measured and cool. "Maybe I should take this one on myself."

The suggestion hit Daniel like a physical blow. The idea of Robert going solo, especially given the dangers they'd faced together, was unthinkable. It was a stark reminder of how close they'd come to fracturing their partnership with a few careless words.

"No, that's crazy," Daniel said quickly, leaning forward with renewed intensity. "I'm with you, let's go."

The words were simple, but they carried the weight of a renewed commitment. Daniel's eyes met Robert's, silently conveying his apology and his dedication to their shared mission. For a moment, the room was silent save for the distant sounds of life outside.

The sunlight that had seemed so warm earlier was replaced with a cold moonlight, illuminating the fine lines of tension on both men's faces. Slowly, almost imperceptibly, Robert's posture began to relax. The edge in his eyes softened, replaced by a glimmer of understanding. He gave a small nod, accepting Daniel's recommitment without words.

As they sat there, the moment of crisis passed but not forgotten, both men knew that their partnership had just weathered a significant test. The doubts Daniel had voiced wouldn't simply disappear, but for now, they had chosen trust and unity over suspicion and division. The path ahead remained fraught with danger and uncertainty, but they would face it as they always had - together.

As they began to discuss the details of their upcoming mission, the familiar rhythm of their planning served to further mend the momentary rift, reinforcing the bond that had brought them halfway across the world to fight for justice in a land not their own.

The time was spent half on discussing their plan of attack, and the other half on putting their uniforms on. The layers of protective leather, belts, shin guards, and carrying cases, as well as their weapons of choice, felt too time consuming. Robert pondered how he could reduce the time it took just to get into their battle fatigues, while Daniel wondered if he looked silly in this Halloween attire akin his favorite vigilante superheroes of his younger days.

The Korean market bustled with nighttime activity, a cacophony of voices haggling over prices mixing with the sizzle of street food and the occasional honk of a car horn. Amidst this chaos, Natasha and Ivan worked furtively, their movements sharp and agitated as they loaded boxes into a waiting van.

"Hurry up, you fool!" Natasha hissed, shoving another box into Ivan's arms. "We should have been gone an hour ago!"

Ivan grunted under the weight, his recent injuries still evident in his pained movements. "I'm moving as fast as I can. These counterfeits aren't going to move themselves, you know."

Their bickering was cut short by a sudden chill in the air. The shadows at the edge of the market seemed to deepen, coalescing into two familiar, dreaded figures. Knightmaire and Demon Knight emerged from the darkness like avenging spirits, their very presence causing the ambient noise of the market to falter.

Without a word, the vigilantes launched into action. The fight was brutal and swift, a blur of punches, kicks, and desperate counters. Despite their best efforts, Natasha and Ivan found themselves outmatched once again. Within minutes, they lay on the ground, battered and barely conscious.

Demon Knight reached into his pocket, a hint of cockiness in his voice as he searched for his calling card. "Does it seem like these encounters are getting easier each time?"

But Knightmaire didn't share his partner's bravado. His posture remained tense, eyes scanning the area with laser focus. "Something is wrong," he growled, his combat stance unwavering.

The words had barely left his mouth when the night exploded into violence. From behind a set of hanging drapes, a mountain of a man erupted into view.

Deathstrike moved with a speed that belied his massive size, closing the distance to Demon Knight in the blink of an eye. The impact was devastating. Demon Knight, caught completely off-guard, was sent flying through the air. He hit the ground hard, the chess piece he'd been about to place skittering across the pavement, a white streak against the dark asphalt.

As Demon Knight lay stunned, the market erupted into chaos. Bystanders screamed and fled, overturning carts and displays in their haste to escape. Knightmaire pivoted to face this new threat, his body tensed for battle. Deathstrike stood like a colossus among the wreckage of the market stalls, his massive frame blocking out the streetlights behind him. His eyes, cold and predatory, fixed on Knightmaire with deadly intent.

In that moment, as Demon Knight struggled to regain his feet and Knightmaire faced down this new, formidable opponent, it became clear that the game had changed. The easy victories of the past were just that - past. Now, they faced an enemy who had not only anticipated their moves but had brought in a player capable of turning the tables. The night air crackled with tension as Knightmaire and Deathstrike sized each other up, two titans poised on the brink of a battle that would shake the very foundations of their secret war.

The night exploded into a frenzy of violence as Deathstrike turned his attention to Knightmaire. The two titans clashed in a brutal dance of strikes and counters, but it quickly became apparent that Knightmaire was outmatched. Deathstrike's raw power and surprising speed overwhelmed the vigilante's practiced techniques.

Demon Knight, shaking off the effects of the initial blow, leapt into the fray. Even their combined efforts, however, proved insufficient against Deathstrike's monstrous strength and skill. The massive enforcer seemed to shrug off their attacks, retaliating with bone-crushing force. Unbeknownst to the combatants, a silent observer watched from afar. Preybird, her eye pressed to the scope of a high-powered rifle, tracked the battle with cold precision. Her finger rested lightly on the trigger, waiting for the perfect moment to intervene.

That moment came as Deathstrike finally gained the upper hand. With a series of devastating blows, he separated the two vigilantes. Knightmaire lay stunned several feet away as Deathstrike bore down on Demon Knight, pinning him to the ground. The enforcer's massive hands reached for Demon Knight's throat, poised to end the vigilante's crusade permanently.

Suddenly, the crack of a rifle shot split the night air. Deathstrike's massive frame tensed, then began to slump forward. He collapsed onto Demon Knight, his dead weight pinning the vigilante to the ground.

"Knightmaire, get him off of me!" Demon Knight's panicked voice cut through the sudden silence.

But Knightmaire's attention was elsewhere. His eyes scanned the surrounding buildings, searching for the source of the shot. In the distance, he caught a glimpse of a figure on a rooftop – Preybird, her rifle glinting in the moonlight before she melted away into the shadows. Knightmaire ducked along the wall, moving towards Preybird's last known position. But by the time he reached the building, she had vanished without a trace. For a moment Knightmaire thought about how effective she was, and that maybe he could learn something from her. But the thought quickly disappeared as he was reminded of all the treacherous and life-threatening actions she had been involved with in the past.

Standing in the middle of the market, surrounded by the destruction of their battle, Knightmaire's posture radiated anger and frustration. Demon Knight, having finally extricated himself from beneath Deathstrike's corpse, stumbled to his partner's side, clutching his head.

"Who was that?" Demon Knight asked, his voice tinged with a mixture of pain and confusion.

Knightmaire's response was grim, a grudging admission that cut to the core of their mission. "You were right... we are over our heads in this."

The market around them lay in ruins, a testament to the escalating violence of their crusade. As sirens began to wail in the distance, both vigilantes knew that the game had changed irrevocably. They had faced their most formidable opponent yet, only to be saved by an unknown player whose motives remained a mystery. As they melted into the shadows to escape the approaching authorities, the weight of unanswered questions hung heavy between them.

Who was Preybird? Why had she intervened? And most importantly, what new dangers awaited them in this increasingly complex web of crime and retribution? The night swallowed them up, leaving behind a scene of carnage and a dead enforcer as mute testimony to the deadly stakes of their mission.

Chapter 13
Han's Deception

The night air was crisp atop the building, a gentle breeze carrying the myriad scents of the city below. Knightmaire stood at the edge of the rooftop, his silhouette a darker shadow against the urban landscape. His vigilant gaze swept over the streets, tracking the ebb and flow of nighttime activity with practiced ease. Suddenly, a familiar figure caught his attention.

Han, the enigmatic informant who had unexpectedly entered their world, was making his way along the street below. His gait was purposeful, his eyes constantly scanning his surroundings - the walk of a man who knew he lived in a dangerous world. Knightmaire's posture shifted, tension coiling through his muscular frame. This was an opportunity he couldn't let pass. Without hesitation, he moved to the edge of the roof, his movements fluid and silent.

With a grace that belied his size, Knightmaire began his descent. He moved like a shadow given form, using window ledges, drainpipes, and the uneven brickwork of the building's facade as his pathway to the ground. Each movement was calculated, born of countless nights prowling the urban Jongle.

As he neared the street level, Knightmaire's mind raced. The encounter with Deathstrike and the mysterious intervention of Preybird had shaken his confidence. Han represented a potential source of answers, a key to understanding the complex game they found themselves embroiled in. The pavement rushed up to meet him as Knightmaire made the final drop, landing in a crouch that absorbed the impact. He straightened, his eyes never leaving Han's retreating form. The street around them was relatively quiet, the perfect setting for the confrontation to come. Knightmaire began to move, his stride purposeful and predatory. He was a hunter now, and Han was his quarry.

As he closed the distance between them, Knightmaire steeled himself for what was to come. This encounter could provide the answers they desperately needed, or it could plunge them deeper into the murky waters of conspiracy and danger that seemed to be closing in around them. The game was about to change once again, and Knightmaire was determined to be the one controlling the board this time.

The night air was thick with tension as Han stumbled into the secluded alley, his hunched figure barely visible in the dim streetlight. His slow, labored movements betrayed his exhaustion or perhaps an injury. Unbeknownst to Han, danger lurked in the shadows. In a flash, a powerful grip seized Han from behind. Before he could react, he was yanked into a small, dark enclosure. The iron grip belonged to Knightmaire, a formidable presence even in the gloom of the alley.

Knightmaire's fingers dug into Han's collar, pulling him close. His voice was a low, menacing growl. "We've been getting shot at. And not by the Russians, but by some assassins."

Han's breath came in short gasps, but he managed to keep his voice steady. "I don't know what to tell you. It's a dangerous life that you lead."

Knightmaire's patience was wearing thin. He jerked Han even closer, their faces now inches apart. The vigilante's eyes glinted dangerously in the dim light. "Who are you really, and how do you know so much about the Russians?"

Sweat beaded on Han's forehead as he stammered out a response. "I just watch them, and want to clean the streets... just like you!"

The air grew even more tense as Knightmaire reached for something at his belt. The metallic glint of a knife appeared, its sharp edge now hovering dangerously close to Han's exposed throat. Knightmaire's voice dropped to a deadly whisper. "I don't believe you, man."

The alley fell silent, save for the rapid beating of Han's heart and the faint echoes of distant city life. The knife at his throat promised that his next words could be his last. The tension in the alley reached a crescendo. Han, his back against the wall and a knife at his throat, let out a defeated sigh. With slow, deliberate movements, he reached into his pocket and produced a worn leather wallet.

"I'm with the Korean Counter-Mafia Task Force," Han confessed, his voice barely above a whisper.

Knightmaire snatched the wallet, his eyes never leaving Han as he flipped it open. The badge inside gleamed dully in the faint light. Knightmaire's eyes narrowed suspiciously. "This is fake," he growled, his grip on the knife tightening.

Desperation etched itself across Han's features. He raised his hands in a pleading gesture, his words tumbling out rapidly. "I swear... call my supervisor!"

With trembling fingers, Han fished out his cell phone. The screen illuminated his face with an eerie glow as he held it up for Knightmaire to see. The vigilante's eyes darted between Han's face and the phone, noting that a call to a ROK police chief was ready to be made.

Knightmaire's jaw clenched as he weighed his options. In one swift motion, he released Han and grabbed the phone. The knife disappeared as quickly as it had appeared, replaced by the cell phone in Knightmaire's gloved hand. His thumb hovered over the "Send" button for a split second before pressing it decisively.

The alley fell silent as Knightmaire raised the phone to his ear. Han held his breath, his fate hanging on this call. A crisp, professional voice broke the silence, emanating from the phone's speaker. "Greater Seoul Metropolitan Police, Special Projects Division. How may I help you?"

The Korean operator's voice echoed slightly in the narrow alley. Knightmaire's eyes widened almost imperceptibly, his gaze locked on Han. The revelation hung in the air between them, promising to change everything. The tension in the alley dissipated as quickly as it had built. Knightmaire abruptly ended the call and thrust the phone back into Han's waiting hand. Han pocketed both his phone and wallet, the gesture almost reflexive after years of police work.

Han's shoulders sagged with relief, but his eyes held a haunted look as he began to speak. "We've been trying for eighteen months to bust the Russians. I've lost my brother and family to this." His voice cracked slightly, betraying the depth of his pain. "Then you come along, and yes, I've turned a blind eye, but you get results.

139

That's what we lack, and frankly, I don't care about due process anymore."

Knightmaire remained silent, his back now turned to Han. The vigilante's voice was gruff when he finally spoke. "Who was shooting at us?"

Han's brow furrowed in concentration, his mind racing through possibilities. After a moment, he ventured, "It may have been Preybird, an assassin hired by the highest bidder from time to time to take care of the ugly stuff. Preybird could have been going after you, and that other man got in the way." Han paused for. a moment, contemplating if his information were a breach of security.

He assumed to take the risk, as it seemed that these vigilantes were his best hope to make the streets safer. "We have been attempting to capture her for quite some time, but she is a most capable threat that is very skilled in blending in."

Without acknowledging Han's theory, Knightmaire began to walk away, his dark figure blending into the shadows of the alley. The distance between them grew with each step.

Desperation seized Han once more. He called out, his voice echoing off the alley walls, "Go to the Russian club! That's where you can defeat the Russians once and for all!"

But Knightmaire didn't pause or turn back. He continued his steady pace, disappearing into the night, leaving Han alone in the alley with his thoughts and the weight of his revelations. As the sound of Knightmaire's footsteps faded, Han was left to ponder the consequences of his disclosure and the uncertain future that lay ahead. The alley, once a stage for this intense confrontation, now stood silent, holding the secrets of the night close to its grimy walls.

The club pulsated with an undercurrent of tension, its opulent interior a stark contrast to the gritty alley we had just left. Russian mafia members, their faces etched with hard lines and cold eyes, filled the room. At the center of it all stood Nicholi, the undisputed leader, his very presence commanding respect and fear in equal measure.

Suddenly, the relative calm was shattered. Iman burst through the front door, his normally composed demeanor replaced by raw panic. He stumbled towards Nicholi, gasping for breath. "Boss, they are here!" Iman's voice was strained, his eyes wide with fear.

Nicholi's reaction was immediate. His face hardened, and he turned to address the room. "Everyone, be ready for what we planned!" His voice carried the weight of authority, and the club erupted into controlled chaos as his men sprang into action. Before anyone could fully prepare, the front door exploded inward. Boris, one of Nicholi's trusted lieutenants, came flying through the air, his body smashing into tables and chairs. He skidded to a stop in the middle of the floor, groaning in pain.

The door hung open, swinging on its hinges, a harbinger of the storm about to break. Two figures materialized in the doorway, their silhouettes backlit by the street lights outside. Knightmaire and Demon Knight stepped into the club, their presence electric. The air itself seemed to crackle with tension as they surveyed the room, ready for battle.

The Russian mobsters tensed, hands hovering near concealed weapons. Nicholi's eyes narrowed as he regarded the intruders, his mind already calculating his next move. The stage was set for an epic confrontation, with the fate of the streets hanging in the balance. As Knightmaire and Demon Knight entered, the crowd of Russians parted like the Red Sea, creating an eerie pathway through the center of the club.

The atmosphere was charged with a mixture of fear and anticipation as the two vigilantes strode purposefully towards Nicholi. Knightmaire and Demon Knight moved with calculated precision, their eyes constantly scanning the room, alert for any sign of trouble. The Russians watched them warily, hands still hovering near hidden weapons.

When they reached Nicholi, the Russian boss raised his hands in a gesture that was both welcoming and mocking. A smile played across his lips, but it didn't

142

reach his cold eyes. "Ah, my newfound friends," he said, his voice dripping with false warmth. "You have been causing me a lot of trouble!"

Knightmaire's response was terse and to the point. "It's time for you and your people to leave."

Nicholi's smile didn't falter. Instead, he made a subtle gesture, beckoning someone from the crowd. "Yes, this may be true," he conceded, "but before I do, please allow me to do you a favor. And then, you tell me if I am the one that should leave."

From the sea of faces, a man squeezed his way forward. Sasha, known to be one of Nicholi's most trusted men, approached cautiously.

Nicholi's eyes glinted with triumph as he turned to Sasha. "Sasha, tell our friends what you saw."

The club fell into an expectant hush. All eyes were on Sasha as he prepared to speak, the tension in the room ratcheting up another notch. Whatever revelation was coming, it was clear that Nicholi believed it would turn the tables in his favor. Sasha looked at Nicholi, nodding in agreement before turning to face Knightmaire and Demon Knight. His voice was steady as he began his tale.

"I was ordered to observe some Korean military prison at the Han River warehouse." As Sasha spoke, the scene around them seemed to blur, giving way to vivid flashbacks of the incident he described.

"I watched as the Korean government was holding a special prisoner in one of their warehouses," Sasha continued. The memory played out before them – a heavily guarded facility, tense soldiers, and an air of secrecy. "Someone attacked the group and rescued the prisoner. I ran away, but then the car passed by me."

The flashback shifted, showing a car speeding away from the warehouse. Inside the vehicle, a figure that wasn't visible before – Han – could be seen removing the hood from the rescued prisoner's face.

Sasha's voice cut through the vision. "As the prisoner was leaving, the hood covering his face was removed. I saw who the government was holding. Now the Korean mafia has him."

Another quick flash showed Sasha on the side of the road, hastily snapping a photo with an iPhone as the car sped past.

As the club came back into focus, Nicholi's voice was grim. "And that man is very bad for business."

Demon Knight, his curiosity piqued, took a step closer to Sasha. His voice was low and intense as he asked, "Who was it?"

The tension in the room was palpable. Knightmaire and Demon Knight stood rigid, waiting for the answer that could change everything. Nicholi's smug expression suggested he held all the cards, while the rest of the

Russians watched the scene unfold with bated breath. Sasha hesitated for a moment, his eyes darting between Nicholi and the vigilantes. The identity of the prisoner hung in the air, a revelation that promised to shake the very foundations of the ongoing conflict.

Nicholi smoothly inserted himself between Demon Knight and Sasha, his voice carrying a hint of amusement. "Ah, but that is the real question. I ask you, do you even know who to trust? I believe that pictures are better than words."

With a flourish, Nicholi produced an envelope and handed it to Knightmaire. "Please, look. I can wait," he said, his confidence evident in every word.

Knightmaire took the envelope, his posture tense as he opened it and withdrew the contents. As his eyes fell upon the photos inside, his body language shifted abruptly, betraying his shock.

Demon Knight leaned in to examine the pictures, his reaction mirroring Knightmaire's. "You can't be serious," he muttered, disbelief coloring his voice.

Nicholi's smile widened, satisfaction gleaming in his eyes. He reached into his pocket and produced a card, extending it towards Knightmaire. "Now, I will leave you to your own devices. Get out, as the sight of you wears down my good nature."

As he spoke, the atmosphere in the club shifted palpably. The Russian crowd began to close in around

Knightmaire and Demon Knight, their movements slow but deliberate. The message was clear – their welcome had worn out. Knightmaire and Demon Knight, still reeling from the revelation in the photos, began to back away. Their earlier bravado was replaced by a wary tension as they retreated towards the exit.

The Russians continued to advance, their faces a mix of triumph and menace. As the vigilantes reached the doorway, the weight of what they'd learned seemed to hang heavy on their shoulders. They stepped out into the night, leaving behind a club filled with smug Russians and a host of new questions. The door closed behind them, but the implications of what had transpired inside would undoubtedly follow them into the darkness. Whatever was in those photos had clearly shaken their resolve and potentially altered the course of their mission.

Inside the quiet interior of a Korean home, Robert sat alone, his face illuminated by a dim lamp as he pored over the photographs spread before him. The silence was heavy, broken only by the rustle of paper as he flipped through the images. After a long moment of contemplation, Robert reached for his phone. His fingers moved with purpose as he dialed a number, his expression a mix of determination and unease.

"Hello, is this the Seoul police?" he asked, his voice taut with tension. "Can I get a hold of the Special Projects

146

Division?" There was a pause as Robert listened to the response on the other end. His brow furrowed slightly.

"Hello, I am looking for a detective Han," he continued, a note of urgency creeping into his voice. Another pause, longer this time. Robert's frown deepened as he processed the information he was receiving.

"There is no detective Han?" The disbelief was evident in his tone. "Can I get connected to the Counter Mafia Task Force?"

As he listened to the reply, Robert's expression shifted from confusion to frustration. His free hand clenched into a fist on the table. "There is no such Task Force?" he asked, incredulity coloring his words. "Don't you have something that investigates mafias?"

The final pause was brief, Robert's patience clearly wearing thin. "No, thank you," he said curtly, ending the call with a sharp press of his thumb.

Robert set the phone down, his gaze unfocused as he processed the implications of the conversation. The photographs seemed to mock him from the table, their secrets now compounded by this new mystery. After a moment of deep thought, Robert's eyes fell on the address card Nicholi had given them. With sudden resolve, he snatched it up, along with his keys. Without a backward glance, he strode out of the house, leaving the scattered photographs behind.

As the door closed behind him, the empty house stood silent, the abandoned photos the only evidence of the turmoil that had just unfolded. Whatever Robert had learned, it was clear that his next moves would be crucial in unraveling the web of deceit that seemed to be tightening around him.

Chapter 14
Renewed Determination

The atmosphere of the dimly lit bar was thick with smoke and the low murmur of conversation. Daylight struggled to penetrate the grimy windows, casting long shadows across the room. A handful of patrons nursed their drinks, lost in their own worlds. At the bar sat Daniel, a figure of dejection and defeat. Empty bottles surrounded him, testament to his prolonged stay. A stark bruise marred his cheek, hinting at recent violence. He stared blankly ahead, barely registering the world around him as he sipped his beer. The door swung open, admitting Jessica. She strode purposefully to the far end of the bar, her eyes sweeping the room before settling on a seat. As she ordered a beer, her gaze drifted towards Daniel.

Recognition flickered in Jessica's eyes, followed quickly by irritation. "You," she said, her voice carrying easily in the quiet bar.

Daniel turned slowly, his face a mask of indifference as he met Jessica's accusing stare.

Jessica's frustration was palpable as she spoke again. "Why do you keep following me?"

For a long moment, Daniel said nothing. The weight of unspoken words hung heavy between them. Finally, he responded, his voice rough from drink and emotion, "What does it matter?"

The tension between them was electric, drawing curious glances from the other patrons. Jessica's fingers tightened around her beer bottle, her posture rigid with barely contained anger. Daniel, in contrast, seemed to sag further into his seat, as if the very act of speaking had drained him. The bar around them faded into the background, the scene focused entirely on these two figures locked in a silent battle of wills.

Jessica sighed, her anger deflating slightly. "I feel the same way," she admitted, her voice softening.

Daniel turned to face her, his eyes searching her face. "Have you ever felt that you were doing the right thing, and it all blows up in your face?"

"Yes," Jessica replied, her response immediate and tinged with a hint of bitterness.

Daniel's shoulders slumped further. "Really? Because I feel like there is no point to what I've been doing lately."

Jessica's expression shifted, curiosity replacing irritation. She moved to the stool next to Daniel, her eyes drawn to the bruise on his cheek. "Is that how you got your bruise? Doing pointless things?"

Daniel brushed his cheek absently, wincing slightly at the touch. He turned back to his beer, avoiding her gaze. "Something like that."

There was a pause as Jessica seemed to wrestle with her thoughts. Finally, she spoke, her voice low and confessional. "I just found out that I may have caused some major trouble as well, and I don't know what to do about it."

Daniel looked at Jessica intently, his eyes suddenly sharp and focused despite his inebriated state. "Whatever you did, you need to make amends, or else it will haunt you the rest of your life."

The weight of his words hung between them, filling the space with unspoken understanding. The background noise of the bar seemed to fade away, leaving them in a bubble of shared regret and uncertainty. Jessica's fingers toyed with the label on her beer bottle, her eyes distant as she absorbed Daniel's advice. Daniel, for his part, seemed to have found a moment of clarity in his drunken haze, his gaze steady on Jessica's face. The scene was charged with a mix of tension and unexpected connection, two strangers finding common ground in their separate struggles. The quiet intensity of Daniel and Jessica's conversation was suddenly shattered by an unexpected interruption.

Robert materialized behind Daniel, his hand clasping firmly on Daniel's shoulder. "Daniel, we have to go," Robert said, his voice urgent and low.

Daniel whirled around, startled and annoyed. "Would you stop doing that!" he exclaimed, his earlier melancholy giving way to irritation.

Robert, seemingly unperturbed by Daniel's reaction, was already moving towards the front entrance. "Come on, I know how to make things right," he called over his shoulder, his tone brooking no argument.

Daniel hesitated for a moment, torn between the connection he'd just forged with Jessica and the pull of whatever mission Robert had in mind. Finally, he stood, swaying slightly as he turned back to Jessica. "Gotta go take care of business," he said, a hint of regret in his voice. "I wish you the best."

With that, Daniel quickly paid the bartender and hurried out the door after Robert, leaving Jessica alone at the bar. Jessica sat there, her expression a mix of surprise and thoughtfulness. The abrupt departure of Daniel and the mysterious arrival of Robert had shifted the energy in the bar. After a moment of contemplation, she made her decision.

"Check!" Jessica called to the bartender, her voice filled with newfound determination. As Jessica prepared to leave, the bar seemed to buzz with unspoken possibilities. The brief encounter with Daniel had clearly sparked something in her, and now she too seemed ready to face whatever challenges lay ahead.

The back area of an abandoned warehouse bathed in the harsh light of day. Two sleek motorcycles stood against a weathered wall, their helmets perched expectantly on the seats. Knightmaire and Demon Knight approached the bikes, their steps purposeful but hesitant. As they neared their vehicles, Demon Knight suddenly stopped, causing Knightmaire to turn back, curiosity evident in his body language.

Demon Knight's voice was uncharacteristically soft as he spoke. "I'm sorry I reacted the way I did the other night. Getting shot at is... it's not what I expected. I..."

Knightmaire cut him off, his voice firm but understanding. "I was scared too. We both know what this means to us, let's finish this."

The tension between them dissolved, replaced by a renewed sense of camaraderie. Demon Knight's mood visibly lifted as he gazed at his motorcycle. "Now this is what I'm talking about!" he exclaimed, excitement creeping into his voice. "We finally get to ride in style!"

"I'm with you...but how do we know where to go?" Demon Knight asked inquisitively.

"That's easy," Knightmaire responded with a silent nod, already donning his helmet. "I followed him after we last met. I know where Han hides out."

The gesture spoke volumes – a mix of agreement, determination, and perhaps a hint of shared enthusiasm. Demon Knight followed suit, putting on his own helmet. The roar of his motorcycle's engine broke the silence, echoing off the warehouse walls. In perfect synchronization, Knightmaire and Demon Knight mounted their bikes. The engines growled in unison, a mechanical harmony that matched the renewed unity between the two vigilantes. With a final glance at each other, they accelerated away from the warehouse. The sound of their departure faded into the distance, leaving behind only swirling dust and the promise of action to come. The empty space where the motorcycles had stood now filled with anticipation for what lay ahead on their journey. The abandoned warehouse stood silent, a temporary sanctuary left behind as Knightmaire and Demon Knight rode towards their destiny.

The thunderous roar of engines reverberated through Seoul's Namsan Tunnel, a 1.5-kilometer artery cutting through the heart of the bustling metropolis.

Knightmaire and Demon Knight, two figures cloaked in mystery and danger, weaved their high-performance motorcycles through the sparse early morning traffic. The tunnel's warm orange lights strobed across their helmets, creating an otherworldly effect as they rocketed past startled commuters. Knightmaire leaned into a turn, his bike responding with surgical precision. He glanced at his speedometer – 120 km/h and climbing. The tunnel's posted limit of 60 km/h was a distant memory. As they emerged from the tunnel's mouth, the pre-dawn skyline of Seoul exploded into view. The iconic N Seoul Tower stood sentinel atop Namsan Mountain to their right, its base shrouded in early morning mist. To their left, the Han River gleamed like a silver ribbon in the faint light, snaking its way through the city's heart.

Demon Knight pulled alongside Knightmaire as they hit Namdaemun-ro, one of Seoul's major thoroughfares. The street was already coming alive with vendors setting up their pojangmacha – small tented stalls that would soon be selling steaming cups of odeng and soju to weary office workers. They weaved through the increasing traffic, the whine of their engines turning heads. Early risers paused in their routines, watching the two riders with a mixture of awe and trepidation. In a city accustomed to the constant hum of activity, Knightmaire and Demon Knight were a discordant note – harbingers of something beyond the ordinary. As they approached Namdaemun Gate, Seoul's Great South Gate and the country's first National Treasure, Knightmaire signaled to Demon Knight. They split up, each taking a different route

155

around the ancient structure. Knightmaire skirted the eastern edge, catching glimpses of the gate's restored wooden superstructure, a phoenix risen from the ashes of a 2008 arson attack. Reuniting on the other side, they gunned their engines and shot down Sejong-daero. The towering skyscrapers of Jong-gu loomed ahead, their glass facades beginning to catch the first rays of sunrise. Among them, the distinctive shape of the Lotte World Tower pierced the sky, a 123-story exclamation point on Seoul's relentless march into the future.

As they approached Gwanghwamun Square, the statue of Admiral Yi Sun-sin stood stoically in the center, his gaze fixed eternally northward. For a brief moment, Knightmaire wondered what the legendary naval commander would make of their high-speed dash through the city he had died defending centuries ago. But there was no time for historical reflection. Their destination lay ahead, somewhere in this sprawling urban labyrinth of old and new, tradition and innovation. Whatever awaited them would have to be faced soon, but for now, there was only the road, the speed, and the awakening city around them.

Seoul continued to stir, unaware that two dark riders were racing through its streets, their mission as mysterious as their appearances. As the sun began to crest the horizon, painting the sky in hues of pink and gold, Knightmaire and Demon Knight pressed on, two shadows moving against the brightening day. As night fell over Seoul, Knightmaire and Demon Knight veered away from the gleaming city center, their motorcycles growling through the increasingly industrial outskirts. They soon arrived at Yongsan Station, once the bustling heart of Seoul's rail network, now a shadow of its former self since much of the traffic had shifted to Seoul Station.

The riders slowed as they entered the railhead, their headlights cutting through the darkness to reveal a graveyard of abandoned rail cars. The air hung heavy with the scent of rust and diesel, a far cry from the neon-lit streets they'd left behind. Hulking shapes of decommissioned locomotives loomed in the shadows, silent sentinels to a bygone era. Knightmaire led the way, weaving between derailed box cars and past dilapidated wooden shacks that had once housed railway workers. Their engines, previously roaring, now purred quietly as if in deference to the eerie stillness of the place. They finally came to a stop beside a graffiti-covered passenger car, its windows long since shattered, leaving only gaping holes like empty eye sockets. With practiced ease, both riders dismounted, the sudden silence amplifying the crunch of gravel beneath their boots.

Knightmaire removed his helmet first, revealing a face etched with determination and the weight of unspoken burdens. His eyes, alert and wary, scanned the surroundings for any sign of movement. Beside him, Demon Knight followed suit, shaking out long hair matted by the helmet. In the pale moonlight, their features seemed carved from shadow, a stark contrast to the colorful tags adorning the nearby train car. Without a word, they moved in unison towards a nondescript entranceway set into what appeared to be an abandoned station house. The peeling paint and boarded-up windows belied its true nature – a hidden sanctuary in plain sight. As they approached, Knightmaire paused, his hand hovering over the door handle. He turned to Demon Knight, their eyes meeting in a moment of silent communication. Whatever lay beyond this threshold would change everything. With a barely perceptible nod, Demon Knight signaled readiness.

Knightmaire pushed open the door, its hinges protesting with a low groan. As they stepped inside, leaving the ghostly railyard behind, the door swung shut, plunging them into darkness. The Seoul night air hung heavy with anticipation as Knightmaire and Demon Knight crouched in the shadows, their eyes fixed on the looming structure before them. The Dangjin Power Station, one of South Korea's largest thermal power plants, stood like a fortress of steel and concrete against the starlit sky. Its massive cooling towers belched steam into the air, creating an otherworldly atmosphere that seemed fitting for the dangerous game they were about to play. From their vantage point on a nearby hillock, they could see two men pacing the perimeter. Even from this distance, their sharp suits and watchful demeanor marked them clearly as members of the Korean mafia, or kkangpae.

Demon Knight turned to Knightmaire, his voice barely above a whisper. "This looks like the right place."

Knightmaire nodded, his eyes never leaving the scene before them. "We need to wait until we see Han. That's the score." He paused, then added with a grim determination, "Be ready for anything."

The tension in the air was palpable, crackling like the electricity generated within the power plant's walls. Both men knew that once they made their move, there would be no turning back. The stakes were high, and the dangers all too real.

Knightmaire suddenly turned to Demon Knight, his face a mask of conflicting emotions. In the harsh glow of the power plant's floodlights, his features seemed etched in stone, but his eyes betrayed a flicker of vulnerability. "If I don't make it out alive," he said, his voice low and intense, "please take care of my sister."

The words hung between them, heavy with implication. It was rare for Knightmaire to show any sign of doubt or fear, and the gravity of the situation wasn't lost on Demon Knight.

After a moment's pause, Demon Knight responded, his tone a mixture of reassurance and determination. "I got your back, man. We can handle this." He clasped Knightmaire's shoulder, a gesture that spoke volumes more than words ever could.

The two men shared a look of understanding. They'd been through countless dangerous situations together, but something about this mission felt different. The involvement of Han, the Korean mafia, and this power plant all pointed to a conspiracy larger than anything they'd faced before. As they turned their attention back to the power station, a sleek black car pulled up to the main gate. The kkangpae guards snapped to attention, and a figure emerged from the vehicle.

Knightmaire's body tensed. "That's him. Han."

Demon Knight nodded, his hand instinctively moving to his weapon. "What's the play?"

Knightmaire's eyes narrowed as he watched Han disappear into the building. "We follow him in. Whatever he's here for, we can't let him leave with it."

With a shared nod of agreement, the two men began their silent approach towards the power station. The hum of the massive turbines inside seemed to grow louder with each step, a fitting soundtrack to the dangerous game they were about to play. As they melted into the shadows cast by the looming structure, both Knightmaire and Demon Knight knew that the next few hours would test them like never before. But with determination in their hearts and trust in each other, they were ready to face whatever challenges lay ahead.

Chapter 15
Han's True Intentions

The first rays of dawn were just beginning to pierce the smog-laden sky over Seoul when chaos erupted within the Dangjin Power Station. The cavernous warehouse corridor, usually filled with the low hum of machinery, now echoed with shouts and the rapid footfalls of dozens of men in sharp suits – the unmistakable uniform of the Korean mafia, the kkangpae. At the center of this storm stood Han, his face a mask of cold fury as he barked orders in rapid-fire Korean. "Move faster! We don't have much time!" His men scrambled to obey, frantically reorganizing crates and equipment, their movements betraying a sense of desperation. From their hidden vantage point, Knightmaire and Demon Knight watched the scene unfold. Their muscles were taut with anticipation, hours of waiting finally about to pay off.

Knightmaire's eyes narrowed as he focused on Han. "There's our target," he whispered, his voice barely audible over the commotion.

Demon Knight nodded, a grim smile playing at the corners of his mouth. "Let's crash this party."

In a burst of movement, they sprang from their hiding spot. The element of surprise was total – before the first shout of alarm could be raised, Knightmaire and Demon Knight were among the kkangpae, a whirlwind of precision strikes and fluid motion. Knightmaire moved like a force of nature, his fists and feet finding their marks with devastating accuracy. A burly gangster rushed him with a crowbar, only to find himself flying through the air, crashing into a stack of crates that splintered on impact. Demon Knight was poetry in motion, his fighting style a deadly dance that left a trail of groaning bodies in his wake. He ducked under a wild haymaker, retaliating with a swift uppercut that sent his attacker sprawling.

The warehouse erupted into pandemonium. The air filled with the sounds of combat – grunts of exertion, cries of pain, the crack of fists meeting flesh. Crates toppled, their contents spilling across the floor. In the chaos, sparks flew as errant blows struck metal surfaces, casting eerie shadows across the walls. Han's eyes widened in disbelief as he watched his men fall one by one to these two intruders. His hand moved to his waist, drawing a gleaming sword from a concealed sheath. The blade caught the harsh fluorescent light, its edge promising swift retribution. As the last of the kkangpae hit the ground, an eerie silence fell over the warehouse. Knightmaire and Demon Knight stood amidst the fallen, their chests heaving from exertion but their stances ready for more. They turned as one to face Han, who stood alone now, his sword held before him in a stance that spoke of years of training.

"Who are you?" Han snarled, his eyes darting between the two men. "Do you have any idea what you've done?"

Knightmaire took a step forward, his voice low and menacing. "We know exactly what we've done, Han. The question is, do you?"

Demon Knight flanked to the side, cutting off any potential escape route. "Your operation ends here," he added, his tone leaving no room for argument.

Han's grip tightened on his sword, a bead of sweat rolling down his temple despite the early morning chill. The standoff crackled with tension, three figures poised on the edge of violence in a sea of fallen bodies and scattered contraband. In that moment, with the rising sun casting long shadows through the high windows, it was clear that the next move would determine everything.

The tension in the warehouse corridor was palpable as Knightmaire and Demon Knight faced off against Han. The Korean mafia boss still clutched his sword, its blade glinting menacingly in the early morning light filtering through the high windows. Knightmaire took a deliberate step forward, his movements measured and controlled. With a swift motion, he reached into his jacket and pulled out a handful of photographs. "We know you are behind everything," he declared, his voice echoing in the cavernous space. Knightmaire flung the photos to the ground, where they scattered at Han's feet like fallen leaves. Han's eyes widened almost imperceptibly as he glanced down at the scattered images. One photo in particular seemed to catch his attention - a clear shot of him behind the wheel of an SUV, his face partially obscured but unmistakable.

But Knightmaire wasn't finished. His voice grew even colder as he continued his accusation. "We also know that the prisoner you broke out was Kim Jong-il, the dead North Korean leader."

At this, Han's gaze snapped to another photo on the ground. This one showed a face in the vehicle next to him - a face that, despite the years and rumors of death, was instantly recognizable as the former North Korean dictator. For a moment, silence reigned. Then, to both Knightmaire and Demon Knight's surprise, a slow, almost fanatical smile spread across Han's face. His eyes, when he looked up from the photos, burned with a fervent light.

"I gladly did what I had to for my dear leader!" Han proclaimed, his voice filled with a mixture of pride and zealotry.

Demon Knight tensed, his fists clenching at his sides. "You're telling us Kim Jong-il is alive? How is that possible?"

Han's smile only widened, taking on a manic edge. "The great leaders of Korea do not simply die. They transcend death itself!"

Knightmaire's eyes narrowed. "Whatever you believe, whatever you're planning, it ends here, Han. You can't possibly think you'll get away with this."

Han's grip on his sword tightened, his knuckles turning white. "You understand nothing! The reunification of Korea under the true leadership is at hand. You are but insects in the path of destiny!"

With those words, the atmosphere in the warehouse shifted. The confrontation had moved beyond a simple case of criminal activity. This was something far larger, far more dangerous than Knightmaire and Demon Knight had initially realized. As Han raised his sword, poised to attack, Knightmaire and Demon Knight exchanged a quick glance. They had come seeking answers, but instead had stumbled upon a conspiracy that threatened to reshape the entire Korean peninsula. The early morning light gleamed off Han's blade as he lunged forward, his face contorted with fanatical determination. Knightmaire and Demon Knight braced themselves, ready to face not just a man, but the dangerous ideology he represented. In that moment, as the clash of steel rang out in the warehouse, it became clear that this battle was about far more than just taking down a criminal. The fate of millions hung in the balance, and Knightmaire and Demon Knight found themselves at the very center of a storm that threatened to engulf all of Korea.

The revelation hit Knightmaire like a thunderbolt. His eyes widened as the pieces finally fell into place. "You aren't the Korean police," he declared, his voice a mix of shock and anger. "You're a North Korean spy!"

Han's face twisted into a sneer, all pretense of civility falling away. "My people will destroy the American infidels and their South Korean lackeys!" he spat, his words dripping with venom and long-harbored hatred.

The air crackled with tension as Han's true allegiance came to light. Knightmaire and Demon Knight readied themselves for what promised to be a brutal fight against a fanatic driven by ideology and misplaced patriotism. But before either side could make a move, the warehouse echoed with the dull thud of bodies hitting the floor. Knightmaire and Demon Knight spun around, only to see two Korean mafia members crumpling to the ground behind them, knives protruding from their backs. In that split second, they realized how close they had come to being ambushed. From the shadows of the warehouse, a figure emerged. Lithe and graceful, she moved with the silent deadliness of a predator. Preybird joined them, her eyes never leaving Han as she took her place alongside her teammates. "Looks like you boys could use a hand," she said, a hint of a smirk playing at the corners of her mouth.

Preybird's lips curled into a smile, a mix of pride and amusement dancing in her eyes. Something in Preybird's expression caught Demon Knight's attention. The intensity in her eyes, the familiar set of her jaw - it all suddenly clicked into place. His realization dawned: Preybird was Jessica. The shock of the revelation must have shown in his body language, because Preybird's smile faltered slightly, replaced by a look of apprehension. Demon Knight turned to Knightmaire, seeking confirmation or perhaps sharing his astonishment.

But Knightmaire's posture told a different story. There was no surprise in his stance, no tension that would indicate this was news to him. Instead, Knightmaire returned Demon Knight's look with a slight nod, as if to say, "Yes, I've always known."

The silent exchange lasted only a moment, but it felt like an eternity to Demon Knight. His mind raced, reevaluating every interaction, every mission, every casual conversation in the light of this new information. How long had Knightmaire known? How long had Jessica been living this double life? Oblivious to the silent revelation unfolding before her, Preybird - Jessica - continued, "I hope I've proved myself worthy of being part of the team."

167

The dynamics of the confrontation had shifted dramatically. What was once a two-on-one standoff had now become a three-on-one face-off, with Han looking increasingly cornered. Han's eyes darted between the three of them, his sword wavering slightly. The fanatical gleam in his eyes, however, only seemed to intensify. "It doesn't matter how many of you there are," he snarled. "The great leader's plan is already in motion. Korea will be reunified under the true leadership!"

Han's lips curled into a cruel smile as he watched Preybird take her place alongside Knightmaire and Demon Knight. "Ah, my little bird has returned to confront her master," he said, his voice dripping with condescension.

Preybird's eyes flashed with a mixture of anger and regret. "You are not my master," she spat back, her hands clenching into fists. "You lied to me. I would never have gone through with breaking that man out if I'd known that it was supporting the North!"

The revelation hung in the air, heavy with implications. Knightmaire and Demon Knight exchanged quick glances, processing this new information about their teammate's past involvement.

Knightmaire, however, remained focused on the primary objective. He took a step forward, his voice low and threatening. "Where are you keeping him?" he demanded, his eyes boring into Han's.

Knightmaire stepped forward, his voice steady and determined. "Whatever plan you think you're executing, Han, it ends here. We won't let you plunge the Korean peninsula into chaos."

Preybird's hands moved to her belt, where more throwing knives gleamed in the early morning light. "Last chance, Han. Surrender now, or this gets ugly."

Demon Knight cracked his knuckles, a grim smile on his face. "Well, uglier."

Han's response was a primal scream of rage as he charged forward, his sword slicing through the air. The Knight Squad sprang into action, their movements synchronized like a well-oiled machine. As the clash of steel and the sounds of combat once again filled the warehouse, one thing was clear: this was no longer just a mission to take down a criminal. It had become a race against time to prevent a catastrophe that could reshape the entire geopolitical landscape of East Asia. The fate of two nations now rested on the outcome of this battle in a nondescript power plant on the outskirts of Seoul. And as the first rays of sunrise began to filter through the dusty windows, illuminating the fierce combat below, the Knight Squad knew that failure was not an option.

But before Han could respond, the tense atmosphere was shattered by the sharp crack of a gunshot. The sound echoed through the warehouse, causing Demon Knight to flinch instinctively. Time seemed to slow as they all reacted to this unexpected turn of events. Han's eyes widened in shock and pain. He staggered backward, his hand clutching his chest where a rapidly spreading crimson stain was blossoming on his pristine white shirt.

"What... who..." Han gasped, his legs buckling beneath him. The sword clattered to the ground as he fell to his knees, his face a mask of disbelief and agony.

Knightmaire spun around, searching for the source of the shot. Preybird dropped into a defensive crouch, her hand moving to her belt of throwing knives. Demon Knight moved swiftly to Han's side, more out of instinct than any sympathy for the man.

"He's hit bad," Demon Knight reported, his voice tense. "But who the hell fired that shot?"

The warehouse fell into an eerie silence, broken only by Han's labored breathing. The Knight Squad formed a tight circle, backs to each other, scanning the shadows for any sign of movement.

"Show yourself!" Knightmaire called out, his voice echoing in the cavernous space.

For a long moment, there was no response. Then, a voice emerged from the darkness, seeming to come from everywhere and nowhere at once.

"Han's usefulness has come to an end," the voice said, cold and detached. "As has your interference in matters beyond your understanding."

Preybird's eyes narrowed as she tried to pinpoint the source of the voice. "Who are you? What's your stake in this?"

A dry chuckle resonated through the warehouse. "My identity is irrelevant. What matters is the game at play here. A game you've unwittingly become pawns in."

Knightmaire's jaw clenched as he realized the full extent of their predicament. What had seemed like a straightforward mission to bring down a criminal had just exploded into something far more complex and dangerous.

Han, still on his knees, coughed weakly. Blood speckled his lips as he struggled to speak. "You... you don't understand. The reunification... it's the only way..."

The mysterious voice cut him off. "Silence, Han. Your part in this is over."

The Knight Squad found themselves in an impossible situation. Their target was critically wounded, an unseen assassin was in their midst, and the simple truths they thought they knew were crumbling around them.

Knightmaire's voice was low, meant only for his teammates. "We need answers, and we need them now. Whatever's going on here, it's bigger than we thought."

Demon Knight nodded grimly. "Yeah, but how do we fight an enemy we can't even see?"

Preybird's grip tightened on her knives, her eyes constantly scanning their surroundings. "We adapt. We survive. And then we get to the bottom of this, whatever it takes."

The sharp crack of a gunshot shattered the tense standoff. Han's eyes widened in shock, his mouth opening in a silent scream as the bullet tore through him. He stumbled backward, his legs giving way beneath him. With a final, gurgling gasp, Han collapsed to the ground, blood pooling rapidly around his prone form. Knightmaire and Demon Knight reacted instantly, their bodies moving with practiced precision. They spun towards the source of the gunfire, dropping into defensive stances, ready for whatever threat might emerge.

"Preybird, check Han!" Knightmaire barked, his eyes scanning the area for the shooter.

Preybird darted to Han's side, her fingers seeking a pulse. After a moment, she looked up, her face grim. "He's gone."

Demon Knight's voice was tense. "So, who the hell just turned our primary target into Swiss cheese?"

As if in answer to his question, a figure emerged on top of a nearby hill, silhouetted against the early morning sky. The man stood with an unmistakable air of authority, a pistol still smoking in his hand.

Knightmaire's breath caught in his throat as recognition dawned. "It can't be," he muttered, disbelief coloring his voice.

Demon Knight squinted, then his eyes widened in shock. "Is that...?"

Standing atop the hill, looking down at them with cold disdain, was none other than Kim Jong-il – the supposedly dead former leader of North Korea.

"Impossible," Preybird whispered, rising slowly to her feet.

Kim Jong-il's voice carried across the distance, filled with contempt. "You thought you could interfere with the grand plan for Korean unification? You are but insects to be crushed under the weight of history."

Knightmaire's mind raced, trying to process this impossible turn of events. The man they thought they were rescuing from captivity had just executed his own operative. Everything they thought they knew about this mission had just been turned on its head.

"How are you alive?" Demon Knight called out, his voice a mixture of awe and fear. "The whole world saw your funeral."

A cruel smile played across Kim Jong-il's lips. "The world sees what we want it to see. And now, you have seen too much."

With a flick of his wrist, armed figures began to emerge from the shadows surrounding the warehouse. North Korean special forces, their weapons trained on the Knight Squad.

Chapter 16
The Real Enemy

Knightmaire's voice was low, meant only for his teammates. "Whatever happens next, we stick together. We're in uncharted territory now."

Demon Knight cracked his knuckles, a grim smile on his face. "Well, they always say it's not a real Knight Squad mission until we're facing impossible odds."

As the North Korean forces closed in, with the presumed-dead Kim Jong-il watching from his vantage point, the Knight Squad stood ready. They were outnumbered, outgunned, and facing a threat they never could have imagined. But as the first rays of sunrise began to illuminate the warehouse, one thing was clear – this was no longer just a mission. It was a fight for survival. Kim Jong-il turned and fled from his hilltop perch, his laughter echoing across the open park near the power station. The pistol that had ended Han's life gleamed in his hand as he ran with surprising agility for a man of his age and supposed death. Without hesitation, Knightmaire, Demon Knight, and Preybird sprang into action, their feet pounding the dew-covered grass as they gave chase. The early morning sun cast long shadows across the park, the peaceful scenery a stark contrast to the high-stakes pursuit unfolding.

The Knight Squad found themselves quickly encircled by the North Korean forces. The air crackled with tension as the three elite operatives stood back-to-back, their eyes darting from one hostile face to another. Despite their extensive training and formidable skills, they knew they were grossly outnumbered. The once-proud Knight Squad found themselves on their knees, hands bound behind their backs. They exchanged grim looks, silently acknowledging the gravity of their situation.

The crowd of North Korean Soldiers parted, and a figure emerged. He walked with the confident stride of a man accustomed to power, his eyes cold and calculating as they swept over the captured operatives.

Kim Jong-il's voice carried back to them, his words in fluent Hangul cutting through the crisp air. "So, you are the two individuals that have been clearing up the Russian problem for us."

Demon Knight, his breath coming in controlled bursts, shot a confused glance at Knightmaire. "What's he talking about?"

Knightmaire's face was a mask of concentration, but his eyes betrayed a growing unease. "I don't know, but I have a feeling we're not going to like the answer."

Kim Jong-il's voice came again, tinged with triumphant glee. "Thanks to Han manipulating you, you took care of all my problems. Now I can resume my conquest of the South, creating a grand Democratic People's Republic of Korea, under my rule!"

Preybird translated quickly. "He's saying Han used us. That our missions... they were part of his plan all along."

The realization hit the Knight Squad like a physical blow. Every operation they'd undertaken, every Russian threat they'd neutralized – it had all been orchestrated to clear the path for Kim Jong-il's grand scheme.

Knightmaire's jaw clenched, his voice tight with suppressed anger. "We've been played. All this time..."

Preybird nodded grimly. "Agreed. Whatever his plan is, it ends now."

Knightmaire, staring down the barrel of the gun, showed no fear. His voice rang out, filled with defiance. "Even if you kill us, there will be others to stop you!"

Preybird stood next to Demon Knight, who remained unnaturally still, his gaze fixed on Kim Jong-il. She straightened her posture, her body language shifting subtly as she turned back to face the group.

Kim Jong-il's face contorted into an exaggerated expression of mock concern, his voice dripping with sarcasm as he responded in Hangul. "No there won't. You see, the Americans and Russians may be against me, but I have many countries that are in my favor... the Chinese, the Iranians, and even the Syrians. All waiting for me to take over this country so we can annihilate the westerners and their allies!"

Preybird translated quickly, her voice tense. The implications of Kim's words were staggering – this wasn't just about Korea anymore. It was a global conspiracy that threatened to plunge the world into chaos. Demon Knight, still oddly unaffected, remained silent, his lack of reaction a stark contrast to the gravity of the situation.

Kim Jong-il's grip on the pistol tightened, his eyes gleaming with malevolent triumph as he continued. "Your days of helping me are over."

Preybird's translation came out as barely more than a whisper, the weight of their predicament settling heavily on the team. Knightmaire's mind raced, searching for a way out. They were outmaneuvered, outgunned, and now faced with a threat that extended far beyond anything they had anticipated. But giving up wasn't an option – not with the fate of millions hanging in the balance.

Preybird's hand inched towards her throwing knives, her eyes never leaving Kim Jong-il. "Whatever you're planning, whatever alliance you've built, we will stop you."

Demon Knight remained eerily still, his lack of response growing more conspicuous by the moment.

Kim Jong-il's finger tightened on the trigger, his voice cold. "You are in no position to make threats. Your interference ends here, along with your lives."

The tension in the air was palpable, the beautiful park setting a surreal backdrop to this life-or-death confrontation. The Knight Squad stood on the precipice, facing not just their own mortality, but the potential fall of nations. As Kim Jong-il's finger began to squeeze the trigger, time seemed to slow.

The tense standoff was shattered in an instant as Preybird's voice cut through the air, cold and determined. "I think not, old man."

Before anyone could react, a shot rang out. Kim Jong-il's eyes widened in shock and pain as the pistol was violently wrenched from his grip by the impact of a bullet. He crumpled to the ground, clutching his injured hand, his scream of agony piercing the morning air. Knightmaire and Demon Knight spun around, their faces masks of surprise and confusion. The shot hadn't come from behind them - it had come from Preybird herself. Preybird stood unflinching, a smoking gun in her hand that seemingly materialized out of nowhere. Her eyes remained fixed on Kim Jong-il's writhing form, her expression unreadable.

"Preybird, what did you do?" Demon Knight exclaimed, finally breaking his unnatural silence.

But before Preybird could respond, the air was filled with the deafening sound of gunfire. The Knight Squad turned to see a horde of men pouring over the top of the hill behind them - the entire Russian mob, guns blazing and faces set in grim determination.

"Get down!" Knightmaire yelled, diving for cover behind a nearby park bench. Demon Knight rolled behind a tree, his eyes wide as he took in the chaos unfolding around them. Bullets whizzed through the air, tearing into the ground and splintering trees. The peaceful park had transformed into a war zone in a matter of seconds.

Preybird, seemingly unperturbed by the hail of gunfire, calmly walked over to Kim Jong-il. She grabbed him by the collar, hauling him to his feet. "Your plan has failed," she said, her voice barely audible over the gunfire. "Did you really think you could outmaneuver everyone?"

David Noble

Knightmaire, crouched behind the bench, tried to make sense of the situation. "Preybird! What's going on? Whose side are you on?"

Preybird turned to her teammates, her eyes glinting with a mixture of determination and regret. "I'm on the side that prevents a global war," she shouted back. "Sometimes, that means playing all sides."

The Russian mob was advancing down the hill, their gunfire providing cover as they moved. Kim Jong-il, caught between Preybird and the advancing Russians, looked less like a mastermind and more like a cornered animal.

Demon Knight, ducking out from behind his tree to fire off a few shots, called out, "So what now? We're caught between a megalomaniac dictator and the Russian mob!"

Preybird's response was drowned out by a particularly close burst of gunfire. The Knight Squad found themselves in an impossible situation - outnumbered, outgunned, and apparently outmaneuvered by their own teammate. As bullets continued to fly and Kim Jong-il struggled in Preybird's grasp, one thing was clear - this was far from over. The park had become a battlefield, and the fate of nations hung in the balance of the chaos unfolding in this once-peaceful corner of Seoul. Amidst the chaos of flying bullets and shouted orders, a new figure emerged, striding purposefully through the mayhem as if he were taking a leisurely stroll in the park. Nicholi Volkov, his presence commanding and unperturbed by the firefight around him, walked past Demon Knight, Knightmaire, and Preybird, his eyes fixed on his target. Without hesitation, Nicholi reached Kim Jong-il, who was still struggling in Preybird's grasp. With a strength that belied his refined appearance, Nicholi grabbed the North Korean leader and hauled him to his feet. Kim Jong-il winced in pain, his injured hand hanging limply at his side as he was forcibly stood up. The once-confident leader now looked disheveled and desperate, a far cry from the mastermind who had been gloating just moments ago. As Nicholi began to turn away with his captive, Knightmaire's hand shot out, firmly grasping Nicholi's shoulder and stopping him in his tracks.

"Where do you think you're taking him?" Knightmaire demanded, his voice steely with determination.

The gunfire from the Russian mob seemed to fade into the background as tension crackled between Knightmaire and Nicholi. Demon Knight and Preybird moved closer, forming a tight circle around Kim Jong-il and Nicholi.

Demon Knight, his stance ready for action, chimed in, "Someone want to fill me in on who this guy is and why he thinks he can just walk off with our target?"

The Russian mob's gunfire had slowed, as it became apparent that the North Korean forces had been defeated.. Kim Jong-il, caught in the middle of this power struggle, looked from face to face, perhaps realizing that his grand plan was unraveling before his eyes.

Nicholi's voice was calm, almost cordial, as he addressed Knightmaire. "You've done well to bring this... situation to light. But I'm afraid this is where your involvement ends. Kim Jong-il is coming with me."

Knightmaire's grip on Nicholi's shoulder tightened. "I don't think so. We've uncovered a plot that threatens global stability. Kim Jong-il needs to answer for his actions."

Nicholi's smile widened, but it didn't reach his eyes. "And he will. But not to you. There are bigger players in this game, my friend. Players you don't want to cross."

A new standoff had reached a critical point. The Knight Squad, Nicholi Volkov, Kim Jong-il, and the Russian mob all poised on a knife's edge. One wrong move could reignite the violence, but the right decision could potentially avert a global crisis. Knightmaire found himself at a crossroads. Did he trust Nicholi Volkov, a man clearly involved in this complex web of deceit? Or did he risk everything to maintain custody of Kim Jong-il?

The dimly lit warehouse fell silent as Nicholi Volkov slowly turned to face Knightmaire. His steely gaze flickered to the hand resting on his shoulder, a rare physical contact that spoke volumes in this world of unspoken threats and allegiances. The touch was both a warning and a reminder – even in this den of wolves, alliances were fluid.

Nicholi's face remained impassive, but his voice carried a hint of resignation mixed with iron resolve. "Even I have to answer to someone," he said, the words hanging heavy in the musty air. "The only person with the power to make sure this is taken care of correctly."

Chapter 17
Enemies and Allies

The Knights Squad tensed, hands inching towards concealed weapons. They'd faced down Nicholi and his outfit before, but something in the crime lord's tone sent a chill through even the most hardened among them. With a subtle nod from Nicholi, the warehouse erupted into controlled chaos. His loyal mafia members, who had been lurking in the shadows, sprang into action with practiced efficiency. The air filled with the metallic symphony of safeties being disengaged and slides being racked. Within seconds, an arsenal of weapons materialized – sleek pistols, compact submachine guns, and even a few Soviet-era relics that spoke to the mob's roots. All barrels trained on the Knight Squad, who found themselves suddenly outgunned and outmaneuvered. The tables had turned in an instant, and the warehouse now thrummed with lethal potential. Amidst this sea of drawn weapons, Nicholi moved with the calm confidence of a man accustomed to walking through storms. He strode past the now-frozen Knight Squad members, each step measured and deliberate. In his hand, he clutched the Kim Jong Il – a small, innocuous-looking device that belied its true significance in this dangerous game of power and loyalty.

As he reached the threshold of the warehouse's side exit, Nicholi paused. He turned back, his eyes glinting with a mixture of challenge and dark promise in the weak light filtering through grimy windows. "Follow me," he commanded, his voice a low growl that seemed to resonate in their very bones, "and you will see."

The invitation hung in the air, laden with both threat and intrigue. It was clear that whoever chose to follow Nicholi would be stepping into a world where the lines between ally and enemy blurred like watercolors in the rain, and where the true seat of power remained shrouded in layers of mystery and danger. As Nicholi's figure disappeared into the shadows beyond the doorway, the Knight Squad exchanged quick glances. Three distinct groups stood in an uneasy tableau: the battered remnants of the Knight Squad, Nicholi flanked by his Russian mob enforcers, and a visibly worse-for-wear Kim Jong Il.

Knightmaire, the de facto leader of the Knight Squad, turned to Nicholi, his metallic mask unable to hide the confusion in his voice. "What is going on?" he demanded, the words echoing slightly in the open space.

Nicholi Volkov's lips curled into a smile that didn't reach his cold, calculating eyes. He kept his gaze fixed on a point in the distance, beyond the assembled groups. "Here he comes now," he said, his Russian accent thick with anticipation.

Knightmaire followed Nicholi's line of sight, spotting a vehicle approaching from the shimmering horizon. The low rumble of its engine grew louder, cutting through the eerie silence that had fallen over the parking lot.

Demon Knight, his armor scuffed and dented from recent combat, stepped up beside Knightmaire. "Who do you think that is?" he asked, tension evident in his gravelly voice.

Knightmaire remained silent, his mind racing through possibilities. Friend or foe? Ally or new threat? The vehicle drew closer, a sleek black SUV with tinted windows that revealed nothing of its occupants. The air seemed to thicken with anticipation. The Knights instinctively tightened their grips on their weapons. Nicholi's men shifted restlessly, hands hovering near concealed firearms. Even the battered Kim Jong Il seemed to straighten up, summoning what strength remained. The vehicle came to a stop, its engine cutting off abruptly. For a moment, nothing happened. The only sound was the ping of cooling metal and the faint whisper of a hot breeze. Then, with agonizing slowness, the driver's door began to open. The driver's door swung open, but it wasn't the enigmatic arrival everyone had been anticipating. Instead, Nicholi Volkov sprang into action with startling speed. He grabbed the battered form of Kim Jong Il, practically dragging the North Korean leader towards the SUV. With a grunt of effort, he yanked open the back door and unceremoniously shoved Kim Jong Il inside. Knightmaire tensed, his hand instinctively moving towards his weapon. But before he could act, Nicholi paused, his head tilting slightly as he listened to something through an earpiece. A moment later, the Russian's eyes locked onto Knightmaire, and he raised a finger to point directly at the armored vigilante.

"He wants to talk to you," Nicholi announced, his voice carrying an unmistakable note of smug satisfaction.

Confusion and wariness warred within Knightmaire as he approached the vehicle. The tinted window on the rear passenger side began to lower with a soft electric hum. As the glass descended, it revealed a face that sent a jolt of shock through everyone present. Sitting in the back seat, exuding an aura of calm authority, was none other than Vladimir Putin, the President of Russia.

"You should go back to your family," Putin said, his voice steady and measured. "My people will take care of Kim Jong Il. This country is safe, for now. You have my word."

Knightmaire's mind reeled. The President of Russia, here? Involved in this? He struggled to form a coherent response, his voice tinged with disbelief and a hint of anger. "What gives you —"

Before he could finish, Nicholi's hand clamped down on Knightmaire's shoulder, pulling him back with surprising strength. "Be thankful you still live," the Russian mobster growled, his breath hot against Knightmaire's ear. "You did good things tonight, despite our differences."

Knightmaire's head swiveled between Nicholi and Putin, struggling to process the rapidly unfolding situation. "But —" he began, only to be cut off by the soft whir of the window rolling up, Putin's impassive face disappearing behind the darkened glass.

With a low rumble, the SUV's engine roared to life. Tires crunched against the asphalt as the vehicle pulled away, leaving Knightmaire and his team standing in stunned silence. They watched as the SUV shrank into the distance, carrying with it Kim Jong Il, the President of Russia, and a mountain of unanswered questions. The Knight Squad exchanged bewildered glances, the weight of the night's events finally crashing down upon them. They had fought, bled, and nearly died – but for what? The true game, it seemed, had been playing out far above their heads all along. Knightmaire clenched his fists, a mixture of frustration and determination coursing through him. As the SUV disappeared into the shimmering heat haze, a heavy silence fell over the parking lot. The Knight Squad stood frozen, their minds struggling to process the whirlwind of events that had just transpired. It was Demon Knight who finally broke the spell, his armor creaking as he approached Knightmaire.

"Let's get out of here while we're still ahead," Demon Knight urged, his voice low and gravelly. He placed a hand on Knightmaire's shoulder, gently but firmly pulling him back from where he stood, still staring at the spot where Putin's vehicle had vanished.

Knightmaire's head snapped around, his eyes meeting Demon Knight's. For a moment, it seemed he might argue, but then his shoulders sagged almost imperceptibly. He gave a curt nod, acknowledging the wisdom in his teammate's words. Preybird jogged up to join them, her lithe form moving with a predator's grace despite the night's exertions. Her eyes darted warily between her teammates and the remaining Russian mobsters, ready for any last-minute double-cross. They had only taken a few steps when Knightmaire suddenly halted. He turned, his gaze locking onto Nicholi Volkov, who stood watching their departure with an air of smug satisfaction. The tension in the air ratcheted up several notches as Knightmaire's amplified voice rang out across the parking lot.

"This isn't over between us," he declared, each word dripping with barely contained fury and the promise of future retribution.

Nicholi's response was a smile that never reached his cold, calculating eyes. "For now it is, young man," he called back, his Russian accent thick with condescension. "Goodbye!"

The dismissive tone in Nicholi's voice seemed to hang in the air, a final insult that set Knightmaire's teeth on edge. He felt Demon Knight's hand on his arm, urging him to keep moving. As they walked away, leaving behind the Russian mobsters and the echoes of Putin's unexpected intervention, Knightmaire's mind raced. The night's mission had been accomplished, sort of. Kim Jong Il was no longer a threat, at least not an immediate one. But at what cost? And what new dangers had they unwittingly stumbled into?

The Knight Squad moved silently through the parking lot, their footsteps heavy with exhaustion and uncertainty. They had entered this night as vigilantes, fighting what they thought was a straightforward battle against a clear enemy. They were leaving as pawns in a much larger, more complex game – one with rules they didn't fully understand and players operating far above their pay grade. Knightmaire, Demon Knight, and Preybird made their way across the parking lot. The adrenaline of the night's events was slowly ebbing away, replaced by a bone-deep weariness that seemed to make their armor twice as heavy.

Demon Knight, ever the one to break tension, turned his head towards Preybird as they walked. Despite the fatigue evident in his posture, there was a hint of playfulness in his voice. "So, you're one of us now?"

Preybird's lips curled into a smile, a mix of pride and amusement dancing in her eyes. She met Demon Knight's gaze, her voice carrying a note of certainty that hadn't been there when the night began. "I think my actions tonight would suggest that."

Demon Knight's chuckle rumbled through his armor. He turned his head, seeking Knightmaire's reaction to this exchange. Their leader had been uncharacteristically quiet since their confrontation with Nicholi and the surprise appearance of Putin. To both Demon Knight and Preybird's surprise, Knightmaire's posture seemed to relax slightly. He turned to face his teammates, and though his face was hidden behind his mask, there was a warmth in his voice that had been absent in the tense moments before.

"Well then," Knightmaire said, a hint of a smile evident in his tone, "let's celebrate. I know this bar we can go to in town."

The suggestion hung in the air for a moment, almost surreal after the life-and-death struggles they'd just endured. Then, almost in unison, the three warriors began to laugh. It started as a chuckle, then grew into full-bodied laughter that echoed across the empty parking lot.

192

As their laughter subsided, replaced by companionable silence, a sense of camaraderie settled over the group. They had entered this night as individuals, each with their own motives and secrets. They were leaving as a team, bonded by shared danger and a common purpose. The sun climbed higher, casting long shadows behind them as they reached their vehicle. Before climbing in, Knightmaire paused, looking at his teammates - both old and new.

"Whatever comes next," he said, his voice carrying a mix of determination and gratitude, "we face it together."

Demon Knight nodded solemnly, while Preybird's stance straightened with pride and resolve. As they clambered into their transport, the events of the night still whirled in their minds. Questions about Putin's involvement, the fate of Kim Jong Il, and Nicholi's cryptic words remained unanswered. But for now, those concerns could wait. They had survived, they had won - after a fashion - and they had emerged stronger.

The motorcycle engines roared to life, and as they pulled away from the scene of their most harrowing battle yet, a sense of anticipation began to replace their exhaustion. They were the Knight Squad, defenders of the innocent, and now, with Preybird in their ranks, they were stronger than ever. The bar Knightmaire mentioned awaited them, promising a moment of respite and celebration. But all three knew that this was just the beginning. The night had been long and fraught with danger, but a new day was dawning - for the city, for the world, and for the newly solidified team of vigilantes who had sworn to protect it all.

THE END

David Noble

CHECK OUT THESE OTHER NOVELS
FROM NOBLE PARK

Knight Squad is based on an independent movie created by Noble Park in 2013. You can watch the theatrical release on many video streaming services and video on demand channels to include Amazon Prime, Tubi, Fawesome, and many others.

David Noble

ABOUT THE AUTHOR

David Noble is a native of Tampa, Florida, By middle school he and a group of willing accomplices started making no-budget action movies, which would transition into a degree in Communications from the University of Tampa. In spite of joining the military, David found time to make several short films, turning to feature films by 2011. Over the years David has written, produced, and directed 'ZYDECO' (horror), 'Knight Squad' (martial arts), 'Secret Within The Sphere' (science fiction), and 'Lost Padre Mine' (adventure). These movies are available on many video streaming services today. David's visual works have been awarded and recognized in over 30 film festivals, some of which he has translated into novellas for your reading pleasure.

Knight Squad